Cold Hard Wind

Dean Hamid

Cold Hard Wind

Copyright @2019 Cold Hard Wind
By: Dean Hamid

All rights reserved. No part of this book may be reproduced in any form or by any means, electronic or mechanical, including photocopying, recording, or by any information storage or retrieval system without the prior consent of the Author, Dean Hamid. Except for brief quotes used in reviews, or by a reviewer who may quote brief passages in a review to be printed in a magazine, newspaper or on the Web. For information contact: DeanHamidPresents at DeanHamidPresents@gmail.com.

This is a work of fiction, any references or similarities to actual events, real people, living or dead or to real locales are intended to give the novel a sense of reality. Any similarity in names, characters, places, and incidents is entirely coincidental. Although the author has made every effort to ensure the accuracy and completeness of information contained in this book, the author assumes no responsibility for errors, inaccuracies, omissions, or inconsistencies herein. Any slight o people, places, or organizations are unintentional.

Editor: Lashonda Johnson/Ghostwriter Inc LLC
Contact Info: Ghostwriterinc2016@gmail.com

ISBN: 172232175X
ISBN-13: 978-1722321758

DEDICATION

*Dedicated to my friend, Jane Pannella:
Cancer sucks!*

ACKNOWLEDGMENTS

My respect to the following for the extra push I needed: Paperback Pushers; Brandie Davis-Urban Books, April Freeman-Book Love and Promotions, Author Tee Blocker, Jane Pannella, Author Brandi Westry, Aaron Sims-BAF Gallery, Author Tee Blocker, Marilyn Brown "SLYCE" The Book Club & 'THE INTERROGATION ROOM', Unique Griffin-The Unique Reading Room, Safi Kweli, Bashawn Pringle, SJS Editorial Services, Chastity Adams, Carla Dean, Tina Shivers-I Am Tina Louise Graphics, Niq Niq's Promotions, La Belle Cuisine, mercury0055, elizwilkerson, oneononepoet, nerdgirlmax, alidapoet_alifreehanddesigns, Wahida Clark, and Florzel Thompson, Dawuh Azim, and Todd Jefferson, Leonard 'Wise' Greene, Spanky, Black Art & Goals. Friends...all. Thank you!

DEAN HAMID

CHAPTER ONE

"Just like your mother…you're good for nothing!"
When she first heard those words, she couldn't quite grasp the gravity of them. At eleven years old, she was way too young. It was only after they yelled at her in an enraged frenzy, over and over again, did she realize it was harmful to her. She wanted to run and escape from it all. It hurt her so much, but she couldn't muster up the nerve…the courage. Accepting the cruel, bitter reality facing her, was useless. In time, she'd grow resilient.

Her hard-working, verbally abusive father would, after a hard day of work, enter their cramped, small, two-bedroom apartment, stomping off to a stabbing-cold and bitter shower to scrub off the dirt and grime that would stick to his body after hours spent in ditches shoveling damp dirt, and sludge. All the while waiting patiently for good curses to emerge.

To him, it never seemed to end. Miles of inner-city terrain laid waste by financial squalor that plagued his home city, and how he loathed every minute. But it was a job, and Detroit, Michigan didn't have many these days. So, when one was available, regardless of what it was, it was well worth doing. The other choice was to be like the masses—broke, hungry, and homeless.

She was this person hidden by her shame. No identity whatsoever except for the books she'd immersed herself into, trying to break free. The remarks from her neighbors as she walked by, was the nerd girl…the geek girl. Thinking she was 'too good for us girl.' Scathing, nasty comments. But, all the while biding her time and saying under her breath, *My day will come!*'

Staying stoic, she continued to strive. She graduated with a

G.P.A. of 4.1 then went on to pursue her goal of getting a degree at the prestigious Wayne State University. It was her escape.

For all the scholastic and academic achievements she'd accomplished, she made it out alive. Out of the unenlightened, mundane existence, many glamorously called, *'the hood.'* For Kim Rashell Williams though, it wasn't soon enough, but finally, her day had come.

Kim's mother had abandoned the home when she was just a small child. Kim remembered her mother's everyday routine. After Kim would arrive home from school. One: she'd bust open a pack of Ramen noodles. Two: whip up some Kool-Aid…orange, Kim's favorite. Melancholic, she remembered how she stroked her hair. Recalled her crying softly, all the while muttering under her breath, like a prayer of sorts.

"Baby, I have to do this, or he'll kill me. You'll understand…one day…" After tucking her in bed and kissing her softly on the cheek, she disappeared completely from her life.

Her father came in later that night in a drunken stupor, his norm. Once he realized Kim's mother was gone, he raised all sorts of hell. He tore up the house, blew a fuse and went ballistic. He frantically searched the neighborhood. Then the following morning, he woke up and accused relatives and friends of hiding her and plotting against him. He burned bridges wherever he went. But she was nowhere to be found. She'd vanished, or as she called it, escaped.

Once he realized what she'd done, he had to switch up, change and get wise—quick. It was either that or give Kim over to Child Services. He couldn't do that, he'd never given up hope that one day, she would come back to him. If not for anything else, then for their child. He'd be there when she did, waiting.

After spending months drowning his sorrows in a bottle daily, he finally gave up hope. DDTs kicked in and hallucinations would come and go. He couldn't hold a job, and he found himself talking to her when she wasn't there. Doing other crazy shit like that. He needed to be able to discern his realities, so, he quit. It was at that moment of clarity when he accepted the reality that she just might not come back to him. For all it was worth, though, he seemed to have grown more miserably, and it was all aimed at Kim.

It made for strange bedfellows because although his rantings directed towards her would become worse. He never stopped her from getting an education. He made sure Kim had clothes, books, pen, paper and whatever else she needed, and that she was at school every day on time. She'd bring home straight As, thinking that would relinquish the tirades, but it didn't. So, she somehow made it work for her, acting like a shield protected her from it all. The price to bear was psychological, for both of them.

So, it was just him and her, and the other one. The one she was always scared of. The toxic, verbal abusive one. But for how long? As long as she continued to educate herself, it was always kept at bay.

Kim stood motionless, staring at this small child with intensity. Brought back to reality from deep within, her flashbacks and anxiety brought on by her own insecurities as a child. Just like the one panic-stricken in front of her now. Hurt, alone, just like she used to be when she was a child.

"Could the child trust her…should she trust her? she asked herself. "Could they even trust each other?" *'My God,'* she thought. *'What was she thinking?'* She inwardly scolded herself.

There wasn't any time for that now. The child's slanted, doe-like eyes stayed affixed on Kim as she continued pondering on what she to do next, and, even what not to do. Everything she'd walked into so far made her want to run, get as far away as she could and erase everything from her mind. But she couldn't just leave this child.

She started toward her cautiously and reached out her

hand. The small child trembled, but hell for Kim, it was no better. She was shaking herself, that only made the small girl even more nervous if that was possible. She had to try to keep her composure. The child pulled back slightly toward the inside of the closet that Kim found her hiding in earlier. She tried prodding her out, by anything other than the compassion in her eyes. She needed her to cooperate. She sighed, she had to desperately figure this whole thing out, it was ugly.

Finally, the child stepped forward, then just as suddenly, she pulled back. She'd heard a sound, Kim heard it also and whirled around with the child hidden behind her back. Eyes fixed on the opened door she now wished she would have closed. Edging inside the closet now, she realized there wasn't much room for them to fit into. She then glanced over at a large dresser to her right. Instinctively, she grabbed the child's hand and eased toward the back end of it into the shadows.

She heard steps climbing up the stairs, heavy and weighted…a man's steps. He wore a black suit, a white, starched shirt with a silk tie. He was Asian and his name was Trang. Kim heard him coming toward the door to the room where they hid. She crouched down, gesturing her hand toward her mouth at the child. She understood and was quiet.

Then, they heard him say, "Make sure everyone is dead!"

"Hell, there's blood all over the damn place!"

They had to get out of there quick. The child wasted no time backing out the window and scurrying over to the flat part of the ten-foot-high building. She stopped and peered over the ledge, then back at Kim like, now what?

Now Trang turned toward the room. He had a hunch someone was around, but he saw no one. "You see something!"

"No, it's clear."

He turned towards another man who was with him, his hand extended, gesturing him back. "Just thought I heard something, that's all."

The man turned back around and asked. "Uh…Trang. You

do want me to check downstairs, right?"

"Uh...yeah," he said as he reached into his pocket and pulled out his cell phone.

The young man he was with had now returned and said, "Nothing, 'cept dead bodies."

"How many again?"

"Eight."

"Damn, eight?"

He turned and looked at him. "All dead?"

"Dead as a door..."

"Yeah, yeah, yeah...doorknob."

He counted on his fingers. "The one in the master bedroom. Two across the hall. Guns in hand... musta been bodyguards. There was the mother, and two kids dead in a back room, near a window, and of course, the two downstairs in the kitchen...servants, perhaps."

"Perhaps?"

"They were trying to get away, but..." He turned his head. "...put up a good fight trying to get away."

"Yeah, away."

"Didn't make it though," he snided.

"Okay, be down in a sec. Gotta call the boss."

The man stopped and turned towards him, smirking. "Tell him it's a bloodbath."

Trang walked over to the window in the bedroom and peeped out. The phone rang on the other side and picked up. "Hello."

"It's me, Trang."

"Why the hell are you calling this number!"

"Look, something happened."

"Well, clean it up, that's why I pay you, people."

"Listen."

"Okay...okay, what!"

He glanced out at the backside of the mansion. Two acres to the rim of the yard, and about one-hundred feet to the side,

there stood a thick row of trees. He stretched his eyes, thinking.
'*There had to be a fence, somewhere in the brush,*' he thought.

The voice on the other end grew impatient and screamed into his phone, "What!"

He snatched it away from his ear and leaned against the window frame. "One… got away."

"One got away? What the hell are you saying?"

"That one got away… a girl."

"You didn't go after her!"

"Don't worry, we'll get her."

"Which one was it?"

"I'll call you later."

"Hey, no, tell me…"

Trang hung up, straightened his coat, then walked out of the room. He turned around and took one last look at the window, then bit his bottom lip. "A problem, always a damn problem," he grumbled. "Which one of them was she? And, what exactly did she see?"

He'd get on it, but right now, he had to go through the motions. He'd find her…soon, dispose of her and the problem then.

CHAPTER TWO

Kim walked over to the ledge where the child stood and peeped over the side, it was a nice drop. The bushes might break their fall. She could possibly do it, but the child. She glanced over at her. She was small, short and didn't look too athletic. The brainy type perhaps, she'd probably break something, and Kim would catch hell. She wasn't trying to carry her. She had to figure something out because they couldn't go back to the room.

Maybe she should go to a cop and tell them what she knew, then give them the little girl. But what about the man in the room? Kim couldn't help but recall the look on his face and wonder if he was involved? Had he seen her face? He acted like a cop himself.

They might ask why she was there. The only person who could back up her story had been murdered along with the whole household. She just knew she'd become a suspect and they'd ask why she left in the first place. After all, this was Detroit, corruption wouldn't be past them.

"No, I'll wait," she told herself.

She figured that she'd go home and make some calls. But first, how was she going to make it to the ground without being all broken up? "Damn," she mumbled.

The child had scooted over to a ledge overlooking some bushes in a corner. There was an aluminum gutter fan across the front of the garage to its sides, and she hung onto it as if her life depended on it. Right now, it did, it seemed like it might have been strong enough to crawl down.

'*How can a child know about all this?*' she thought and shrugged it off. This was their ticket.

The tiny agile little girl hugged onto the gutter and knelt, bracing her leg against the well as she did. It was like she was an old pro. Like she'd done this a million times before.

'Had she?' Kim thought as she inched halfway down.

The child paused, looking up at Kim as if to say, *'Come on.'*

Kim bounced out of the daydream she was in and fell in right behind her. She made it to the ground and waited. Kim was hesitant though and started moving slowly and scared. Sensing this, the little girl climbed back up to where she was and helped to brace her feet as she coached her to the ground. Kim nodded her head toward the girl and smiled. After all, she'd underestimated her. But what else did this child know? She reached out for her small hands, they were trembling. She grabbed them and pulled her closer.

"Alika... tell me, what happened?"

Alika stared up at the window, then back at Kim. Tears welled up in her eyes and shock came across her face. Kim knew what it was, she'd been there. Alika suppressed all that had happened because, during all the commotion and trauma, she didn't have time to process it. Or didn't know how, until now, so naturally, she started to crash.

All of a sudden, they heard the crackling of tree rubbish coming from around the side of the long garage. The child picked up on it. They both looked over at the edge of the bush line to their right and hauled ass. Diving through, they hit the ground and rolled. Other than crickets singing their late-night tunes, they made not a sound. The men upstairs shined their lights their way but didn't see anything. They shrugged and kept moving. Kim breathed a sigh of relief, then picked the child up and ran. Where they were running to? She wasn't sure. Why they were running in the first place? She wasn't sure. But there were enough dead bodies in that house to convince her to get far away.

Who killed Malana, her friend and the rest of the family? Why leave the child? Or did they even know they had? She approached Woodward Avenue and spied the long, expanding thruway. She could make it across Palmer Park and into the suburbs. Then hopefully find a cab and get to her apartment, asap. She'd have to make some calls, and figure out what the hell was going on because right now, a whole family was murdered. Except for the little girl who may or may not have seen anything, or everything, with her riding shotgun. Yeah, she was clueless, that was never good.

****

Over drinks at the Savoy Hotel in London, Tho Hoang Tran first heard about Detroit's potential, and soon after flew in from his home in Laos. He remembered being berated by an airport customs agent who told him he was crazy to want to invest a penny in the city, much less a dime, but he did.

The fifty-four-year-old retired as a top executive of the multi-national Cargill, then spent his liquid assets to buy, along with his partner, Tommy Hong, 150 homes to refurbish and rent. He was among one of many investors that bought rock-bottom properties in Detroit. Tran fell in love with it, and the money.

It was like a gold rush, he thought as he looked out the window of his penthouse office overlooking Woodbridge. He wore the reserved, casual clothes of old-school business, a dark suit, wingtip shoes, and cuff links. Reaching over his desk, he picked up a glass partially filled with age-old Remy, took a sip, and put it down. He sucked in air to cool the hot, warming liquor as it went down his throat. Nodding his head in approval, savoring its flavor, he tilted his head back, then heard a knock at the door.

"Who is it?"

"Lam."

"Come in, Lam."

The short, small, pint-sized man came through the door and stood in front of the desk. He wore a scraggly black polyester shirt with a thin, black tie and black jeans. He pulled at the tight leather jacket he wore, trying to conceal the automatic he had holstered underneath. Playing with his hands, he waited for his presence to be acknowledged. Finally, Tran did.

"How did the job go?"

The man pulled at the neck of his collar nervously. His large Adam's apple bobbed up and down as he took a breath. "Uh, okay, boss!"

Tran turned around, and reached for his drink, keeping his eyes fixed on the man as he reached over his desk. He nodded his head some and sat on the side of it. Then he reached behind him into a drawer. That move made the man in front of him jumpy.

Tran paused, looked up then pulled out a humidor and opened it. He offered him a long Cuban cigar. "Want one?"

The man nervously replied no. Right behind him, stepping through the door were two other men. They were large, bodybuilder status at best. Tran directed them in. The man in front of him became highly agitated, increasingly more nervous.

"You wanted us, boss?" they asked.

"Yes, Jung." He smiled, then lit and pulled on the cigar, blowing the smoke out, puffing lightly. "You see… Lam."

"Yes, Dai Low."

Tran got up and walked towards him, close enough so he could see the sweat rushing down his head in gushes. He walked around him, sizing him up. Without warning, he grabbed him from behind in a choke hold. Too light in the ass to fight back, Lam reached for his bread and butter, his gun. Jung grabbed at it and twisted it out of his hand. Now, he was defenseless, the big men easily wrestled him to the desk and threw him down on his back, causing him to grimace in pain.

He looked up and yelled, but it was useless. "Nooooo."

Tran had pulled the cigar from his mouth and jammed it into his eye, screaming at him. "You Cambodian, fake-ass gangster. You didn't see the fucking girl!"

"No…no!" He wriggled around in pain as the others held

him down.

Tran pulled the cigar from his burnt eye and reached into his pocket for a light. "You used to have two good eyes, no excuses. How could you not see the girl, huh?"

"I did as you said! Me…the crew, we went in with the…"

Tran jammed the now lit cigar into his other eye. "Two fuckin' good eyes! And, missed her…you should have seen her!" He let him up, and he convulsed around on the floor in pain. Tran pointed to his men and ordered, "Get him out of here!"

The bodyguard looked over at him and asked, "What do you want us to do with him?" They picked him up, dragging him out the door.

Tran turned around and said, "Kill him."

The same suit and tie, slim-figured Asian man named Trang stood at the door, moving Tran's men aside as he came through. Shaking his head in disgust, he stepped into the room and called out to Tran, "What the hell is wrong with you?"

Tran picked up a white, linen cloth and wiped his hands with it. "Wrong?"

"Yeah, what is wrong with you…you crazy?"

He pulled out the chair from his desk and sat. "One… got away."

"We'll get her!" the man said as he hurried to his side. "They thought they took out everyone."

He spun the chair away from him and looked out the window. "We shouldn't have fucked up."

"Yes, you're right, but we still don't kill one of our own."

He raised his hand up. "Okay!" He spun the chair back around and looked at him. "Let that fuck live. We're going to need him anyway to find…the girl."

"Okay, then, I'll have our people keep an eye out for them. Can you call the guy we know? He might know something. What's his name again?"

"Sabo…Vincent Sabo."

"Isn't he with…"

"The Asian Gang Unit."

"Yeah-yeah…" He turned and walked toward the door. Before he grabbed the knob to turn it, Tran called out, "Trang."

"Yeah."

"Keep an eye out, personally."

He smiled. "I will… after all, I know how to use both of mine." He smirked and walked through the door. Tran spun the chair back around, reached into a humidor and pulled out another smoke. Looking at it, he laughed aloud, lit the cigar, turned back around in his chair and reached for the phone. "May-May, call a meeting."

CHAPTER THREE

Her eyes rolled up and down the small Android phone screen searching frantically, for names and people she could call, anyone she could trust to talk to, right now. Someone who could tell her what to do, that's what she needed. Some damn good advice.

She thought about calling Malana's family, but who? Hell, they'd murdered them all. Least the ones she knew, and if she were to call anyone else, too many questions would come up. Like one: why did you leave? Then, she'd end up having to answer that very same question for the police. Maybe even to the same police detective that spied her going out of the window but, yet, didn't stop her.

"Oh, hell no." she had to think fast. "Who?" Her eyes fell on a name-Vong…Vong Nguyen. "Of course!" She definitely could trust him.

Granted, all he wanted to do was get in her pants, but right now that was her upper hand. She needed him to make runs without being seen and help her find out what was going on without exposing her own hand.

"Yeah, I'ma have to call his horny ass." She smirked. "He's the only who can help."

Distracted briefly by Alika eating Ramen noodles at the kitchen table. Alika, for the most part, was on her own and Ramen noodles was all she had to eat. For Alika, it didn't matter anyway. Ramen noodles was a popular dish in Asian culture and around her own home. So, she feasted and wiped her mouth with the back of her sleeve, then she got up from the table, eased over to where Kim sat and started peaking over her shoulder. Kim was still busy scrolling through Malana's page on Facebook. She paused to hit other friends and look through photos. She saw Malana with her husband, Malana with her kid,

Malana with what she guessed were her inlaws, she knew for sure that they weren't her parents because she knew them. Then she took another look at Malana's husband, Vien and his friends. She saw Vien at work, Malana and Vien at a work function that looked like some sort of party.

"Them!" Alika shouted, pointing at the small, brightly lit screen.

Kim turned. "What!"

"Them!" Alika gasped, pointing at two men standing behind her parents. "Them!"

"What about them, Alika?"

"They were there…"

"They were there…what?" Kim quickly clicked on the photo to download, and Alika trembled. Kim pulled her close and hugged her. "Don't be scared…don't worry."

Those were the right words from her, but inwardly, she didn't have a clue what was about to happen. She was scared her damn self. What would she do with this child? She knew she had to keep her safe though, for Malana. But damn, where could she take her, except to the police?

****

"Okay, now, tell me again. You were called by Malana… and?" Vong sat on the side of the brown leather, worn-looking sofa she had tucked off in a corner of her small, but modest two-bedroom apartment.

The soft, brown leather complimenting the tan, silk throw pillows sitting neatly behind a cherrywood coffee table. He'd just got in from work and was still wearing a suit. He was rather tall for an Asian male and slim with long legs.

Vong had just kicked his shoes off and swung his feet around on the tabletop when Kim yelled out, "Hell no…get your big ass feet off my table!"

"Damn…" Vong said as he sucked his teeth, feeling

almost like a child being scolded by his mother. He scooted further back into his seat with his arms folded. "So."

She focused back on the story. "Malana had called me that afternoon. Said she needed me to come by her house later that evening." She walked over to the sofa. paused, reflected back then continued. "Hell, I had no problem with it. I mean, we were cool…like sisters." She sat on the sofa opposite him and briefly turned towards the living room area.

An enclosed place surrounded by candles, huge floor pillows, and in the middle of the floor sat a giant flatscreen TV. There sat Alika right in front her eyes were glued to the anime cartoon she was watching. She turned to them and smiled briefly.

Kim turned her attention back towards Vong, and said, "I was busy. You remember we had that Xaykosy meeting?"

"Oh, yeah, big boy millionaire from Laos."

"Yeah," she said, rolling her eyes. "Didn't really trust him though."

"So, you were supposed to go to, Malana's. Then, what happened?"

"Yeah…yeah, I didn't get the chance to call her. Let her know I was going to be late. Remember, you know, we got bogged down…crunching numbers."

"More like kissing ass…"

"Anyway, we went out for drinks after it was over…"

"Trying to cool things down."

"Didn't work." She snickered.

She got up and walked towards the small miniature bar she had set up opposite the sofa. She pulled out a half bottle of Bourbon and raised it toward Vong. "Want a drink?"

"Sure…"

She poured two glasses, walked back over to the sofa and handed him his. Then she sat with her legs crossed as she took a long sip and exhaled as the warmness of the hot drink soothe her insides.

"After I left you guys," she continued. "I took a company cab over to the house."

"House…hell, she lives in a baby mansion."

"Yeah, well…house…mansion, whatever."

"Wish I had friends with mansions."

Kim rolled her eyes and said, "You do, Vong, they probably just don't invite you over."

"Smart ass," Vong smirked.

She reached out her hands soothingly. "No… I didn't mean it like that. You just hang out with some very snooty people. People who have money…that's all." She knew she'd touched a nerve.

Vong took a swig, then spat back, "I'm tryin' to get mine. You got to be able to rub elbows with the right people. The rich… movers…shakers."

She wanted so bad to say. kiss ass, but it wouldn't have helped matters any. She waited patiently for him to finish his rant.

"When I arrived, Vong, I didn't notice anything strange. The lights were on, cars were in the driveway. There was nothing unusual, until…until…" She looked off and said, "No one came to the door."

"So…" he said, hunching his shoulders.

She turned his way, looking into his ignorance, she explained the significance. "Check it, Asian culture one-o-one. When you have money, your class changes…your status. You've got servants, and believe me, you don't answer your own door. It's almost like, an insult to the servants. It's that serious."

"Really."

"Damn, right, anyway, I pushed at the door, and it opened wide, then I saw it…"

"Saw what?"

"The blood."

Vong curled in his seat and leaned closer. "You call the

cops? You should have called the cops."

"I probably would have, but I followed a trail…a trail of blood."

"*A trail of blood…* damn."

"It looked like someone tried to run…get away."

"How'd you know that?"

"Bullet holes…I saw the bullet holes, then a big blood splotch."

"Oh, shit."

"I started to haul ass then, but all I could think of was Malana. So, I started up the steps slowly."

Kim stepped back and leaned against the wall, swirling her drink around her glass. "It's funny, but it was like this scene from a horror movie or something. Like I was in it." She made the face of one of those unfortunate actresses in the film. Her eyes were wide, her mouth was open, and she kept her hands out in front of her. Vong was amused so he smiled as she took another drink.

"You know how you know everything you're supposed to do when you're watching, you know." She glanced back over at Vong, walking towards him, and sat, still with the theatrics. She played with her glass in her hands. The show was over, and reality was sinking in. "I just went up the stairs, blood was on the walls. Everything in my mind screamed out, *'haul ass.'* Run! But, I went up the stairs anyway, like…"

"In the movies, Kim, you were in a daze."

"Yeah, Vong." She looked up at him. "I was in a daze."

"So, what happened when you got up the stairs?"

She stared off, her mind was out there now, in an abyss. One that only she could see, but she came out of it just as quick. "I knew where Malana's room was. And, the kids' room. I'd been there a hundred times or more. Instinctively, I went to the kids' room though." She stared down at the floor, recollecting. She took another drink and put the glass down on the table. Tired of playing with it already. A frown curled up on her face. "It was ugly."

"You don't have to..." Vong said, beckoning her to stop.

"Thanks, Vong." She turned towards Alika and said, "She...had two siblings."

"So... you left, right?"

"No, I made the mistake of going into Malana's room. Maybe, I should have...gone to the police."

Vong reached out and grabbed her hand and gently rubbed it. Trying to ease her sorrow, but he couldn't help but notice how soft they were. He almost forgot where he was as he nodded his head, listening. She eased it back. He was catching feelings. She needed to use Vong, and not show him any affection so early on. Vong, however, just thought of it as pure concern and shook it off. He was very well aware of why he was there anyway.

"You don't have to continue..."

"No, I need to...I need to see if I missed anything."

"Okay then."

"I headed towards Malana's room and steeped in. There she was, sprawled out on the floor. Hmmm, seemed like she was pointing towards..."

"Towards?"

"Oh, nothing, I went over, picked up her head and tried to wake her, but she was already dead. The big, bloody hole in her chest only confirmed the worst. I started crying, freaking out and shaking, that's when I heard it."

"What?"

She turned her head towards Alika. She must have gotten bored with the whole cartoon thing because she was now peering out of the window. She seemed to have been waving at something...birds perhaps.

"We... we..." She kept her eyes peeled on her, something wasn't right. "The man with a skinny tie saw us... Asian."

"Man...skinny tie...what the hell are you talking about?"

She turned her head sharply towards him. "The what?"

Cold Hard Wind

"A man with a skinny tie, c'mon Kim... you trippin'?" He snapped his fingers in front of her face.

Just then, she heard Alika yell out, "Daddy's friend...daddy's friend!" Kim turned quickly, Alika had poked her small head back inside the window and beckoned for her to come. "Come... look...daddy's friend!"

That's when she spotted it, the red dot in the middle of her small forehead. She hurriedly sprang out of the chair and darted toward her. She dived on her small body and rolled, covering her up. She let loose only after Alika pushed her up off her. Vong was still glued to his seat with his mouth open, shocked.

She yelled at him. "Get down on the floor!"

He did as he was told and dived to the ground. "*What the hell is going on?*" he shouted.

Kim put her finger to her lips, quieting him. She slowly got up and eased toward the window. She got on her knees and peeked out.

The street below was quiet, up the block was the older lady she'd recognized, walking her dog, a small, overdressed Yorkshire terrier. There he was, looking dead in her face. The doorway came across from them. He was a slim, black-haired Asian man, dressed in all black, the same damn skinny tie, a pair of jeans and cheap, rubber shoes. The same man from the house, he smirked, then nodded. Kim ducked her head quickly. He wanted her to see him, she peeked up again after about a minute, and he was gone. She got up and ran toward her room to search through the closet for large duffel bag.

Vong was right behind her. "What just happened...*what did you see!*" he shouted.

Alika sat on the floor, dazed like she was when Kim first found her.

"I got to go, he'll be coming up here!"

Vong grabbed her and pushed her up against the wall. She struggled, he eased his grip on her arm and screamed. "*What the hell is going on, Kim?*"

She continued to tussle, but it was useless. Vong looked into his eyes and she answered, "I really don't know, Vong. All I know is I got to go. I'll be in touch, trust me!"

"Where are you going?"

"I can't tell you that…yet." She yanked out of his grasp and picked up the bag. She grabbed some clothes, rushed into the bathroom and grabbed some hygiene products. She rummaged through her drawer for certain documents she knew she'd need like, credit cards and cash.

Then she hurried into the living room and barked an order towards Alika, "C'mon!" The child quickly got up and ran toward her. Kim turned back around and looked at Vong. "Don't stay here long, I'll call you."

"How…when?"

"I got all your numbers…all of them."

"*All of them?*" '*Even his people's numbers?*' He snapped out of the thought and nodded. "Okay."

The door slammed and Kim was gone.

He walked over to the window, looking up and down the street. He didn't no one…no Kim. "They must have gone out back," he said, scratching his head. He grabbed his jacket and noticed her laptop, still on. He walked toward it and stared at the screen. "She never logged out." He thought about the consequences as a sinister smirk appeared on his face. "The hell with Kim…all my numbers, we'll see."

Kim had just eased out the back door, she looked through the parking lot of the privately-owned condominium she lived in. It was quiet, she glanced at the opening toward the back side of the enclosed parking lot.

'*Suppose whoever it was that pointed that rifle laser dot at Alika's head was still out there, waiting,*' she thought shaking her head, then she peeked down at Alika who clung to her leg. She had to make a move fast, so she started for another opening. '*The other side of the lot perhaps.*' But she couldn't budge, her legs wouldn't move. What move to make…where? "What the hell do I…"

Alika pulled at her hand, Kim looked down at her. Her small hands pointed towards the opening of the backside where Kim had first looked and said, "Home…"

DEAN HAMID

CHAPTER FOUR

The aura around the room would have been quiet, if not for the ramblings of the old, grey-haired Asian men smoking rolled-up cigarettes and fat cigars. Smoke permeated the air and old-style, custom-made suits, crafted post-50's era was the attire. They sat at a cherrywood, thick, French provincial-style, thirty-foot-long table. The table sat six on each side comfortably. The room had the decor of old-world Orient styling, paintings of small villages, dragons, and Mandarin chinagraph penciled writings hung ornate along the walls, giving it an authentic Eastern flare of sort.

Stilled, black and white photos of families wearing tattered clothes, with toothless smiles. They were all farmers, living, working, and dying, on rice farms perched obtrusively overlooking the vast, sprawling hills of Laos. A closer looked showed that the same man seemed to appear in them all. An elderly, bent-over man of Asian descent.

The lore was that this very man had been a Chut Suk, an *'advisor-for-life.'* In some cultures, he'd be a lord or a don. For a century or more, generations and generations of his family had followed the tradition of the powerful triads and prospered. These lithographs served as a sinister sense of that proof. Tran walked over to one of those framed portraits and smiled at the photos of his grandfather posing with these villagers. He pulled out a white handkerchief from his dinner jacket, wiped off some dust and beamed.

Then stepped back and admired them all before turning toward the steward. "Clean them when we're done in here."

"Yes, Master Tran," he answered.

Tran nodded his approval and directed his attention toward the gentlemen that had gathered. He then snapped his fingers at his hired men toward the door and waved them off. They stepped back, and the doors closed behind them. He made his way to the head of the table, pulled out his chair and looked steel-eyed at each and every one of them before he sat. "Gentlemen, the meeting will convene."

Immediately, the murmurs and small talk ceased. They all turned their attention toward him and silently waited patiently for his next words. They were waiting for a statement…a command? It didn't matter, because whatever the rhetoric, regardless of what he said, his words were acted upon. Just like it had been in his family since his great-great-grandfathers, for centuries.

He was descendent of the Hip Chong Tong, and he was holding the strongest position in the Laotian community in America, he was simply, the boss.

"Oh…" He gestured toward the photos. "Afterward, we shall take photos as… a reminder." A sneer formed ominously across his lips.

The older men sitting around the tables nodded their approvals quickly. It seemed they also had a stake in those ancient, antiquated photos on the wall. Those poor, weather-beaten, rough faces that Tran Tong had ruled over were after all their left behind family members.

The room got eerily quiet as Tran paced the floor for a moment before speaking. Once he reached the head of the table, he began, "I gathered you all here so we can discuss business at hand." He walked toward a board and flipped it around, on it was a graph. On the bottom left end, a red line halfway across gradually raised upward toward the middle, then plunged sharply starting a rapid nosedive. Everyone's attention was directed at the board as he spoke. Then, pointing towards the descending line, he continued, "This was a bad moment. We agree?"

The men all nodded profusely. They were aware of the situation. "But, fortunately, we caught it in time." He flipped the board around again and another graph was shown. This one had the red line pointing upward all the way across. "Better days are forecasted." One gentleman raised his hand and Tran turned his attention towards him. "Yes, Mr. Hong."

"The problem has been...eliminated then?"

Tran smiled. "Of, course...eliminated."

All the other older men looked at each other in agreement, grinning, except this one gentleman. He was younger than most of them, in his early fifties perhaps. He smirked, looking around at them all, then back at Tran and said, "How do we know...for sure?"

Tran was infuriated, he abruptly turned towards the man. "For sure...you questioning...me?"

"Questioning you...yes! There is a lot of money on the line. I'm sure that a simple question like that could be answered quite easily. No disrespect, of course."

Tran raised an eyebrow. "How dare this man come here and try to disrespect me like this," he asked himself.

But, he could, he was Vinny Ta's man. He reported directly to him. A grin slowly eased across Tran's face as he calmed himself. He looked off from him at the other men that waited in anticipation for an answer.

"Of course not." He walked back over to the board, covered it up, and flipped it over. He then turned around and continued, "I can assure you, the problem was eliminated." His attention was directed at Sen Hong as he made it clear. "Is that good enough."

"I'm sure, Tran." Sen Hong raised his glass above his head and gestured. "A toast...to a prosperous year!"

As the gentlemen threw back their wine, Tran took the opportunity to ease around the table toward Sen Hong. He bent over and whispered covertly in his ear, "You know something I don't?"

He snickered and nodded at the rest of the gentlemen who were totally oblivious to the sidebar conversation they were having. Sen Hong slowly set his chalice down and turned toward Tran, looking him dead in his eyes and snickered again.

"Well, let's put it this way, I better not."

Tran was nothing to play with, but Sen Hong wasn't either. They'd both worked for the same man at one time, the Chut Suk. Sen was sent to America years ago right behind Tran, and he kept track of him. It was unspoken, but Tran knew. He kept Hong or at least tried to keep him out of the business' personal business, especially the stealing money part of the business.

Tran needed a front man to do that. That's where Alika's father had come into the picture. He'd helped Tran launder hundreds of thousands of dollars, easily. Alika's father, Vien knew it was a risk. If Vinny Ta ever found out, his whole family would be dishonored. So, he had to for the sake of his family, not let them know, especially his wife Malana.

The Hip Chong Tong needed sufficient confirmation to act on any foul play in regard to money. To accuse Tran without that was akin to treason. Especially, since Tran had so much power. Alika's father was that proof, but it was leaked what he was doing, resulting in the hit. But Alika's father was no slow leak, he held a bank deposit box at different banks with secrets, ledgers and account numbers. He knew the danger of it, so, he never mentioned to the others where they were.

He, Tran, or the Hip Chong Tong. One random individual could not get to the numbers, it was next to impossible. It still didn't stop Tran from trying Alika's father though and torturing damn near everyone in the house trying to get them, but he got nothing. Everyone in the house was murdered. He had an idea where to look next, but that's all it was so far…an idea.

As for the Hip Chong Tong, they had gotten wind of such numbers. They had to get them quick; many people would be exposed. Time was wasting, it wouldn't be too much longer before Tran would figure it all out, then try to use that leverage for his own gain.

CHAPTER FIVE

Kim caught a cab about three miles out of town and booked a hotel. It was an old, run-down, shabby place, but with all the drama she was involved in right about now, it was good enough. She'd grabbed a few things when she left her apartment but didn't have anything Alika's size. She had three credit cards, she thought maybe that would remedy the situation, but she was unsure.

"They might have a flag or a trace on us," she said to herself.

It was already risky enough using one for the room, but she didn't have enough cash on hand. She only had just enough for the food she'd bought. She shuffled through the cards, thinking about her being ignorant of the ins and outs of the debit card industry, even though she owed money to its cause. The biggest question was could they track them? She didn't have a clue, but she had to make a call. She had to find someone that knew these things. She had to ask questions, like *How to go on the run? Where to go on the run?*

She also had to get clothes for Alika quickly. It was getting windy, and a nip in the air signaled cold winds from across the water out of Canada. She turned towards Alika who was squatting in front of the TV watching cartoons. Kim balled up her face and thought to herself, *'At least I could have changed her shirt or washed out the clothes she had on and given her a bath. But damn, everything happened so quickly!'* Her mind deduced.

"Alika, sweetie…time to take a bath."

She frowned just like any other kid would when pulled away from a cartoon to take a bath. Kim smiled as she walked toward her.

She reached down to grab her hand gently. "C'mon, girl, you smell a little musty." She tickled her.

Kim noticed that for the first time that a smile had eased

across Alika's face. Malana would have been proud of her resilience, she was strong. Kim figured that was a result of her mother. She'd met Malana during Freshman year of college, both seemed liked strangers in the new environment. Neither had any real friends or anyone to talk to. They were called *Nerd Bae*, but upon meeting each other, they bonded. Being that they were both shy and introverted, they shared stories about each other's lives.

Kim's home life was very different from Malana's and much harder in comparison. Malana had the silver spoon, but her ethnicity held her back. It was really hard for an Asian girl to excel in families where the men were held higher in esteem. But she remained persistent in getting an education on a higher level. Even though she knew it would be difficult for her to actually use it. She was expected to look pretty, have good etiquette, and make babies and so she did just that.

They graduated in the top twenty-five of their class but went separate ways so far as school was concerned. They always kept in touch though. It was easy; after all, her husband worked at the same firm as Kim. They were always in and out of each other's lives. She even remembered when Alika was born. After that Malana went to Laos to be with her family for a while. A long while, it seemed. When asked, she always kept her Laotian family affairs regarding those trips private along with Alika. That was strange to Kim, but she didn't pry.

Her plans were to make some calls to some thug friends of hers in Detroit. As she sat on the bed, she frantically searched through numbers of contacts she still had from her old neighborhood of people she stayed in touch with. Her father still stayed in their old home. She hadn't been there to see him in a long while. She hardly ever called, but every now and then, she'd touch base with Ms. Mary, his neighbor, to find out how he was doing and if he needed anything.

She had love for him, of course, he was her father, but he had issues and whenever she went to see him, all he wanted to do was talk about her mother. His early stages of dementia didn't help matters any either. Finally, she'd found a number and a name.

"Damn." she grimaced. "Of all the numbers...Denita's."

Denita was cool and all, but their relationship wasn't built on friendship. She was gay, and Kim's first real attempt at a sexual encounter. Needless to say, it was not a good experience. Not because of her being gay, but because she wasn't shit.

Alika ran into the room, breaking her thoughts, and pointed to a plate of noodles. She hauled ass and wolfed them down. It tickled Kim. Alika's back was wet and still partly uncovered. Kim could see some markings.

"Was she abused!" Kim asked herself curiously.

She walked over to her and asked her to lean forward so she could see better. Alika stood up with a fork in her hand and backed towards the wall.

Kim was perplexed. "It's not that serious, baby." But, evidently, for Alika, it was.

Alika backed up against the wall, trembling with her fork pointing towards Kim and her eyes fixed. This made Kim stop dead in her tracks, she could see the fear in her.

"Such a young child," she mumbled silently. She felt for her. That's what they shared in likeness...fear. "Alika...I'm not going to hurt you." Still, Alika wouldn't budge, her small hands shook from the weight of the fork and the fear that coursed through her hand. "Please, put the fork down, sweetie," Kim pleaded.

It wasn't working, she had to think quickly. She stepped over to her bag and pulled out her phone. Then she pulled up something on the screen and she showed it to her. "See...that's me, I'm not going to hurt you."

Alika's eyes stayed fixed on the image in front of her, then the fork fell from her grasp and hit the floor. Kim quickly picked it up as Alika reached for the phone. A smile appeared on her face, but then as quickly, tears welled up in her eyes. It was a photo of her mother, Malana.

"Mommy," she said as she fell to her knees with the phone clutched in front of her. Tears littered the screen as she caressed the face of her mother.

Kim eased over to her and kneeled. "I miss her too… it's gonna be alright."

But was it? Kim didn't have a clue as to what she was getting into. What Malana had wanted her to accomplish. She hugged her, and Alika gently nudged her backward. Not uttering a word, she turned around and pulled up her shirt, baring her back.

It looked to be a tattoo, Mandarin marking of some type. She looked closer, but it was way too complicated for her. She placed her hand on it and ran her fingers along the lines. Indeed, some were tatted, but there were lines burned in.

She shuddered as she felt them. "Who would mark…much less brand a child?" she asked herself.

They had to mean something not to mention these thugs wanted her bad enough to kill people. Malana had deliberately kept her safe for a reason. That was probably what she wanted to talk to her about when she called.

"Damn," she sighed.

It was too late for that now. She had to find out what those writings meant. *But where and from who?*

****

Vong cut off the laptop, then stretched and leaned back in the chair. As nosy as he was being, he couldn't find anything in the files that was of any use to him. Even though he'd checked out some provocative photos of Kim, otherwise nothing. He figured he'd go back home and make some calls. Suddenly, he heard the door opening.

"Maybe she forgot something," he said to himself and turned around.

Cold Hard Wind

His eyes grew wide with shock as she realized that he was facing the muzzle of a rifle pointing at him from the doorway. He scrambled to the floor just as the screen on the laptop exploded from the gunshots. His heart damn near jumped out of his chest.

He was scared as he hollered out, "Don't shoot…I don't live here…"

More shots riddled the chair he sat in. He hugged the floor quickly and crawled toward the window as more shots followed him. There was no giving up, surely there were going to kill him. He looked back at the desk where he sat it was riddled with bullet holes and torn apart. There was definitely no giving up or he was dead. He peeked his head up, two men in black eased from around the corner. They were looking over at the area, they hadn't spotted him, yet. He stayed quiet and breathed shallowly. They walked past him as he hid beneath the desk, toward the glass and debris on the floor.

He glanced over at the window, he couldn't remember whether there was a fire escape or not.

"Should I chance diving through it?" he asked himself.

Then he had to ask himself if he'd survive the fall four stories down. Then, he glanced over at the door. They were already inside the apartment, now searching the back room. Maybe, he could make a run for the door through the kitchen. One of them backed out, then turned in his direction.

"Did he hear me…see me?" he rambled.

He had, he tapped the other on the shoulder, and that was enough time to prompt Vong to make the decision to run. He made a mad dash for the kitchen as bullets followed behind him. He couldn't stop now, he had to keep his head up and continue moving. He bumped into appliances as he ran determined not to let nothing slow him. He'd hit his shoulder and his knee, the pain registered in his head, but he couldn't stop.

Pop! Pop! Pop!

The loud noise of the bullets behind him, the tearing up of the walls, as well as fear, wouldn't let him stop. He made it to the door and threw himself through and down the steps, falling head first. The tumbling down the stairs hurt bad, as he looked up at the door hearing them coming. As much pain as he was in, he managed to get up. He looked at the door going and hurried outside. He knew it was a stretch, they could get him easy, but there was a wide-open path in front of him.

He exhaled and then screamed, "Fuck it!"

The door flew open, and a man in a trench coat busted in and looked down at him.

"Damn, too late," Vong grumbled. He just knew he was dead, he closed his eyes, waiting for death to come.

Instead, he heard, "Get your fucking ass up and come on!" He opened his eyes at the man reaching out his hand toward him. "C'mon!"

Vong came to his senses and his feet, but the men upstairs in black were already at the door. They littered his path with lead. The man in the trench coat had a gun too. It looked like a cannon to Vong. He pointed it up at them, and all Vong could hear was loud booms clapping in his ears. That prompted him to move his ass, and he dived out of the doorway. The man in the trench coat helped him up and pointed toward a car. They ran toward it and dived in just as the two men ran out the door. He cranked the car up and screeched into the street away from the building. Vong was folded up in the front seat, breathing profusely.

He looked up at his unknown hero and said, "What the hell happened…who are you?"

The man looked over his way and smiled. "Right now…your goddamned savior!" He reached into his pocket, and Vong twitched. The man laughed harder, shaking his head. "My name is Trang, don't be scared now."

The dark-blue sedan pulled up at the opening of an abandoned warehouse on Detroit's east side. They got out of the car, and Vong looked around at the squalor.

"Why'd we come here?" he asked himself.

He looked over at the still unidentified man who went to the trunk and opened it. He took out a black, large leather briefcase. That was weird, but Vong's mind continued to ponder.

His mental ramblings were interrupted when he tugged at him. "C'mon…let's go inside."

"Uh…why are we here?" Vong asked.

Trang walked to the door of the rusted building and pulled out a key. But before he put it in, he turned facing Vong. "Whoever it was that was shooting at you will be looking for you."

"Uh, okay. But, why do we go to a precinct or something?"

Trang half-smiled at him then turned back towards the door. "You can't trust it, they might look for you there." He put the key in, the door popped open and dust shot out from around its edges. He grabbed at the handle to push it open, then stopped and asked him, "You do want to be safe, right? I mean, I can drop you back off where we just left. If you want…"

Vong's mind went back there, and he thought about it, but not too long. His knee still throbbed as pulses of pain shot through his shoulder. He definitely wanted to be safe. Besides, this guy had just saved his life. He had to be safe. "No… no… you're right, no problem."

Trang pushed open the door to the dark murkiness of the insides of the building. Glass littered the floor, and Vong could hear the crunching sound of it as he followed Trang's lead. He was led into a back area, there were lights and another door. He stepped behind Trang and there were Asian men. Men that looked like the ones shooting at him. Trang stopped and pointed him towards a chair. Vong hesitated and started to back up, but three men closed off his path.

Trang smiled at him and pulled out a cell phone. "C'mon,

now, sit, it's okay. They're not going to hurt you…trust me."

Vong hesitated slightly but did as he was told. One of the men offered him a cigarette, and he turned it down. He, however, accepted the stiff drink offered next. His body relaxed as he drank the smooth, warm liquid. The place had electronic surveillance equipment. Hard drives sat on a table in front of him, and as he stretched his eyes more, he noticed about six men inside there with him, all with guns. He also spotted a battery charger with cables and a couple of batteries attached.

"Maybe, they got a vehicle somewhere," he mumbled.

As the liquor entered his system, he relaxed more, and his body became lucid. He seemed to be under some sort of control.

Trang approached him talking to someone on the phone. "Yeah, he's here." Vong wanted to say something, anything, but his mouth appeared to be locked. "I got him from her apartment." He backed up, now standing over Vong as the fluid coursed through his body. His mind swirled round and round. Trang asked him a question, "What is your name?"

Vong's mouth quickly opened and he spat. "Vong Edwards." It was like he wasn't in control. This made him wonder what the hell he was drinking. Was it some kind of truth serum? Right then, he knew he'd fucked up. He should have surrendered to the men who came in. But they were the ones shooting at him.

Trang, running his mouth, answered that question. "Those stupid muthafuckas thought you were with us and started shooting. Almost killed you, too." He laughed.

Vong thought Trang was his savior…the cavalry but no, he was the devil in disguise. He stood over him and pulled out his phone. "I'll be there as soon as I find out what he knows and where the girl went."

Vong's mind screamed. "*I don't know!*"

It was useless, the fist landed on the side of his face as Trang continued to yell at him. "What the fuck did it look like, you bastard!"

Vong's mouth spat things from his memory that even he couldn't control. He tried stopping it, but he was at Trang's mercy. He picked up the cables, turned on the battery charger and clapped them together.

"Where did they go!" was the last thing Vong remembered as his mind went black.

Tears ran heavy down his face. The sparks coming from the cables mixed with his flesh filled the air and his nostrils. Trang tortured his body, and the serum flowed through his veins and his mind.

DEAN HAMID

CHAPTER SIX

Denita looked over the marking on Alika's back, she moved closer in deep thought. She walked over to a library that had books of different languages across the globe and started searching through them. She paused at one, glanced over at Alika, and pulled it out. She flipped through the pages mumbling under her breath. Then motioned for Kim to come over and laid the book down on the small coffee table in front of her.

"Right there." She pointed to a page.

Kim looked closely. "I don't understand."

Denita smirked and waved Alika over. "Watch this." She pointed to the Mandarin markings on the page, and Alika smiled. "Recognize?" Alika nodded. Denita looked at Kim again. "You see?"

Kim shrugged her shoulders and looked at Alika curiously as she beamed. "To tell you the truth, no...still don't."

Denita shook her head at Kim's ignorance. She handed Alika the remote and pointed to the television. "Here you go, knock yourself out, kiddo." She turned her attention back to Kim. "Have a seat." Kim pulled up a seat in front of her. "Okay...the language is Asian."

"Well...I can see that."

"No, silly, it's not that simple. It's old-world Asian, Vietnamese, from back around the Dong Son era...Kings, Emperors, and all that stuff."

"So, what does it say?"

"It's not so much as what it says, it tells a story."

"A story?" She glanced over at Alika. "That small little old tattoo."

Denita laughed again at her unfamiliarity. "Not a whole story, it's like a parable. What's on her back is the ending of a riddle, a piece of a puzzle."

"What does it say?"

She reached into her pocket and pulled out her cigarettes. "Now that, I don't know, I can only tell you the syntax."

"And, what's that?"

"Laotian."

"*Laotian?*"

"Yeah, across from Vietnam."

"Okay, okay, that's where Malana was from."

"Who?"

"Malana…her mother."

Denita lit up the cigarette and blew smoke rings in the air over her head in thought. "I probably might know someone who knows someone."

"Okay."

Denita looked her up and down then leaned forward, touching her thigh. "But…"

Kim twitched but didn't move. "It's not like that."

"Like what?" Denita answered as she moved her hand further up her thigh. "You know, I never treated you bad, Kim! I took care of you." She stood up, walked behind her and leaned over, rubbing her shoulders. "It can still be…"

Kim pushed her hands away. "No!" She stood up and called over to Alika. "Alika, let's go!"

Denita waved her hand at her. "No, Alika, matter of fact, there's a bigger TV in the room. Why don't you go in there? *Now!*"

Alika hauled ass into the room, but not before looking at Kim who sat helplessly in the chair. "Go ahead, Alika," she coaxed.

"Now." Denita walked in front of her and kneeled. Her hands moved towards Kim's plump breast. "Where were we?"

"Please, Denita…no." She tried to push her hand away.

Denita pushed it back. "What…no!" She pushed up on her. "Now, you listen to me, bitch! You came to me for help, or so you say. Now, I know you didn't think this shit was gonna be

Cold Hard Wind

free!"

"I thought you would help." Kim looked away. "I can leave." She struggled to get up.

Denita smacked her. "Sit your ass down!" She walked toward the bedroom where Alika was and peeked in, then closed the door. She walked slowly back toward Kim while unbuttoning her shirt. "You might as well do the same because you ain't getting out of her without giving me some of that pussy...*period*!"

Kim stared at her, fuming. She didn't come there for that, and really wanted to be as far away from that whole scene as possible, but she needed to know about the markings. She also peeked over at the door and without a sound, Kim lowered her head and started unbuttoning her blouse.

Denita was now standing over her half-naked. "Yeah...good girl, just like old times."

Kim wasn't sleeping as she peeked over at Denita who was out cold, snoring. She eased towards the edge of the bed then stopped briefly hearing Denita snort. Not wanting to wake her, Kim waited until she heard the snores again before easing off the bed from underneath the covers. She picked up her clothes and tiptoed quietly towards the door, she opened it ever so quietly and eased out.

Falling back against the doorjamb she let out a sigh of relief and breathed profusely. She had to calm herself down, and after some deep breaths, she focused on the room Alika was in. She opened it slightly and peeked in. Amazingly enough, Alika was still up, watching cartoons. She snickered at her and caught her attention. Alika started to smile and say something, but Kim put her finger to her mouth, motioning for her to not say anything. She pointed to her clothes and told her to put them on as her mind and ears continued listening for any sounds coming from Denita's room.

Once Alika was dressed, she kneeled in front of her. "Okay, I need you to be quiet, we're leaving. Can you do that

45

for me?"

Alika nodded her head and Kim jumped. She heard a sound coming from outside the room. They hid near the closet. Kim crept over to the door gradually with her ear up against it…nothing, so far. She opened the door, and they both slid out. Kim turned toward the living room, looked around and saw what she was searching for…the book. She grabbed it off the table, tucked it in her bag and started toward the door. She unlocked it silently, then opened it, and she and Alika ran down the hall toward the stairway.

About halfway down, Kim peered back up, she was pissed off about what Denita put her through…she trusted her. Tears welled up in her eyes, but then she felt Alika tugging at her. She looked down to find Alika hugging her leg. Kim reached down and kissed her on the forehead. Then they proceeded down the stairs. She opened the staircase door leading outside, peeked around making sure everything was safe, and she and Alika darted out into the early morning, making their escape.

Denita stood by the window watching as Kim and Alika hurried up the street. She shook her head smiling, then walked over to the bed. She sat, reached for her cell phone and dialed some numbers.

Once the person on the other end answered, she said, "Okay, she's got the book…now what?"

"Don't worry about that, you did good…real good." The person on the other end started to hang up.

Denita intercepted, "Hey, what about the payment?"

"Oh, the payment, of course. You'll get what's coming to you, I promise."

"Okay."

Denita tossed the phone on the bed and walked into the bathroom to turn on the water for a nice hot shower. She thought of all the things she made Kim do. How much she had enjoyed it, and how she hoped she'd get another chance. She was clueless as the bathroom door opened until it was too late.

Cold Hard Wind

Two holes tore through the shower curtains, she looked down and saw the water run red. The blood was spurting out of two holes in her chest, and she felt her legs getting weak. She tried reaching for the shower pole but missed and crashed down to the floor. The hot water splashed against her body. Not feeling the heat of it anymore, the deathly coolness crept over her body as she blacked out.

The figure who'd fired the fatal shots reached in and turned the water off. The assailant then pulled back the curtain, turned and walked out as steadily as he'd come in.

****

Sergeant Sabo had just sat in his office. The Asian Gang Unit seemed to be at a standstill, wasn't much shaking or happening. But he did know from his contacts that the girl he sought after was in high demand. Still, he didn't know why. The community among the Yakuza and the locals, kept their mouths shut, even the young gangs that ran Madison Heights, Detroit's Chinatown. But he had to know, why someone would kill a whole family? What was worth that? It didn't matter at first, he got paid regardless. He wasn't supposed to even give a damn, but when he saw the children, it changed the game for him.

He spazzed on his own ass for not getting there sooner. He looked for clues, something about this mass killing was different. The man of the house wasn't a boss. What was that important to kill him and his family and the *servants*? One thing he did know, one of the kids were missing. Did she get away, or, was she snatched up by the killers?

He looked over the papers on his desk. They were frequented names and areas, then he looked over his contacts and still found nothing. Seemed like every time he asked questions about it, they got away from him. Almost as if someone was warning his contacts to clam up. He peered around the police office, but who?

His partner rushed in and threw another paper on his desk.
"What's this?" he asked.
"A homicide...Eastside."
"Why us?"
"Apparently, someone witnessed having company the night before. A black girl...and a little Asian kid."
Sabo snatched up the paper and read the report, then got up and rushed for his coat. He looked back at his partner and yelled, *"What are we waiting for!"*

CHAPTER SEVEN

Vong wriggled fruitlessly in the chair he was tied up in, against a two by six wooden beam. He struggled at the cord around his hands as it bit hard into his flesh. His legs and knees were cramped as the cord burnt into them. He did manage to get a little tipping of the chair motion started. He was putting in work. His chest was singed from the hot cables placed against his skin, as he was tortured into giving up information he didn't have. His only mistake was being nosy and knowing Kim. He still struggled with the whole thing as to why they wanted her anyway, but right now, he could care less. He had to get free.

He stretched his ears listening to the silence still around him, listening for anyone. There was no one, the drugs they'd shot into his veins made him weak, and he threw up. That only made it worse as he continued to struggle. The chair continued to tip as he strained more, but now, he had the rocking thing going. He continued at it, and the more the chair tipped, the more the rope tightened against his chest. It eased its way up toward his neck, threatening to choke him, but still, it continued to loosen, just a little bit.

If the chair tipped over completely, there was a possibility he'd choke to death. Hell, he had to try, so, he continued rocking for the better part of an hour or more. Then finally, he fell over, the rope indeed did slip up to his throat, and get tight, but not tight enough. The back of the chair broke, he extended his legs as he fought with the rope to get it down to his ankles.

"It worked," he said to himself.

The ropes around his arms loosened, he was almost there. He got his hands free, so he pushed at the bottom of the chair. It was happening for him, finally. Then, after a brief struggle, he was just merely taking the rope from around him. He grasped at the pole as he stood himself up. Now, he had to get the hell out of there. He fumbled around in the darkness and felt the steps leading upstairs. He slumbered forward toward them, and that's when he heard the voices at the door upstairs.

He hid underneath the steps, listening. The door opened, and the voices grew louder. They were Asian. He shook his head in disappointment. He damn sure wasn't trying to go through the bullshit he went through again. He searched around and spotted a wooden two by four at the bottom of the stairs to the side. He cautiously grabbed at it and eased it toward him.

'Put all your strength into it, Vong. You've got one shot,' he thought.

The Asians walked down the steps and when they got to the bottom, they glanced over at the wooden beam Vong was supposed to be tied up to.

One of them shouted in Asian that Vong was sure as hell had to be. "Aw, shit!"

He turned and rushed back up the stairs. Vong stepped around and tripped him up, then swung. He caught him upside the head, and he fell backward. The other looked his way, then reached into his jacket, possibly for a gun. Vong swung at him and caught him square in the jaw. He dropped down to his knees, but he wasn't out. Vong swung again, but this time, he missed.

The man was large as well as quick. He reached out and caught Vong by the leg, tripping him. Vong fell, and the Asian quickly jumped on top of him and started choking him. Vong managed to reach out and over for one of the broken pieces of the chair before he went unconscious. He found something, he grabbed at it and with everything he had, jammed the wooden stake-like piece into the chest of his assailant. He fell on top of him, dead.

Vong pushed the Asian off him after a minute, trying to catch his breath. He got up and crept over to the stairs and listened. When he didn't hear anything, he eased up the steps. At the top, he peered out and saw he was still in the garage. He saw a car, he looked in and saw the keys were still in the ignition.

"Probably belonged to the Asians that came in," he said.

He jumped in and started it up then eased out. He stopped and looked both ways, and when he saw that the coast was clear, he hauled ass. He didn't exactly know where he was, nor did he care. All he knew was that he was free.

****

Kim deduced now that she was being followed. She had to keep moving. Whoever it was seemed to be getting closer. Who exactly was after her? She had to factor in that they were also the ones who killed Malana and her family, most likely trying to get to Alika. Something that had to do with the markings on her back, she bet.

She had to find someone to help her and tell her what it all meant. She walked into the supermarket in dark shades, with her hair tied up in a bun and a cap pulled down over her face. She made a half-assed attempt at being discreet to pick up some items for Alika. She loved Ramen noodles in the pack, and Kim found out quickly that they were cheap as well. She ate them herself.

She turned her head abruptly, feeling as if someone was staring. Her paranoia caused her to dip into another section, not thinking that maybe a cart full of Ramen noodles wasn't strange enough. As she turned around again, sure enough, someone was behind her. Panic took hold, but she had to pull it together. Alika was back at the room she'd rented and if she left her there too long by herself, there was no telling what would happen. She couldn't lead whoever was following her back to her.

She dipped around a corner again, and it was the same. She glanced over to her right at the door leading to the stockroom and thought maybe she could escape through there. She dipped in and hid. The door slowly opened as she watched the person who'd been following her creep in. All she could see at first was a shadow of a man. He looked around and headed toward her.

"Maybe, he saw me," she mumbled silently to herself.

She spotted a piece of broken wood from a pallet with a sharp edge. Immediately, she picked it up and grabbed hold of it. The person now was upon her, so she jumped up and swung the stick. He ducked, barged into her and held her down. Then she kicked and screamed.

He hollered out, "*Hold on, Kim…it's me*!" She kept swinging. "*Calm down*!" he shouted.

She opened her eyes, and it was Vong. "What the hell!"

"I wasn't sure it was you." He held her down until she calmed herself. "I'm sorry."

She looked at him and the bruises on his face. "What happened?"

He helped her up. "Come on, let's get out of here."

"Where are we going?"

"Hell, I thought you had a place, I've been hiding out in a car!"

"Come on!" She grabbed him by the hand, and they ran out of the store.

****

"Oh shit!" Vong exclaimed as he flipped through the pages of the old, worn book. "So, those writings are on her back?"

Kim moved closer toward him and leafed through some pages, then pointed out one in particular. "Uh huh, these…right here."

"It says something about Vietnamese folklore in the captions."

"I believe that's what it is, but from another era perhaps." Kim leaned back. "I honestly believe it has something to do with a code."

Vong also kicked back, crossing his legs. He thought for a minute then snapped his fingers. "I think I know a guy!"

"Who!"

"Remember when I first came on the job. They stuck me in the mailroom. I mean…I don't see why they would have put me there…"

"Vong!"

"Oh, yeah, well…" He leaned forward and looked out. "There was an Asian guy. He was young but had an old-school flair, so he always talked about his country like it was some fantasy Hobbit shit or something."

"Okay…okay…where is he now?"

"I don't know, honestly. Once I left the mailroom, I didn't see him anymore."

Kim stood and paced. "Do you think we can find him?"

"We'd have to get an address, but I don't know anyone."

Kim stopped pacing and stared at him. "What?" She smiled. "We might have to sneak in…"

"Sneak in where? The job…you muthafucking crazy!"

She sat next to him and pleaded, "It can be done, we know all the ins and outs. I mean, you're good with computers."

"Yeah." Vong sighed. "I could get in the mainframe."

"Well, then… let's do it." She got up and ran into the bathroom.

Vong called out, "Today?"

Kim turned to where Alika was sleeping and replied, "Maybe not…I have to find someone to watch her."

Vong shook his head. "Damn, okay, I think my mom might keep an eye on her."

"Didn't you say you might be watched?"

"I did, but my mom is something different."

"Different?"

"Trust me, she'd know if someone was watching her, or the house. She's very…different."

"Schizophrenic?"

Vong looked down to the floor. "Yeah, yeah."

Kim moved closer to him and reached for his hand. "Okay, it's cool. Will it be okay to go to her…I mean, the last minute?"

He looked up at her and answered, "We'll definitely have to make sure no one's watching us. And, we can't let her know nothing."

"Okay, that's the plan. I'll play the role of your girlfriend, right. Act like we're going on a date, and I couldn't find a babysitter."

"Oh, great, she'll like that. I'll never hear the end of it either." Vong sighed.

"Okay, tomorrow."

"Sounds good, I'll have the chance to call her and make the arrangements."

Kim stopped and leaned back against the small hotel dresser, then Vong asked her? "Can I stay for the night?"

She looked at him and pointed to the other bed. "Bed's wide open."

"Okay, cool then, we sleep…"

"We…we, my ass!"

Vong smiled, then chuckled. "Well, I knew it wouldn't be that easy."

Kim laughed with him and stepped into the bathroom. She turned on the water in the sink and let it run, splashing the wetness to her face. She looked up in the mirror. Her face still had a shine to it, even after all she was going through. But she noticed slight anxiety marks along her forehead and small bags under her eyes too.

"I gotta get it together," she said to herself.

There were still so many questions to be answered. She had to figure this whole thing out and get Alika to safety. Then, figure out her own next move. It was all too much. She took a deep breath and walked over to the shower to run some bath water. The hot steam poured out from the small, tiled enclosure, and she inhaled deeply. She felt invigorated as the water entered her nostrils. Slowly, she peeled off her clothes, stopped the running water, and stepped into the tub. Immersing herself in, she leaned her head back, getting comfortable. The next thing she knew, she was fast asleep.

Vong leaned back on the bed, wondering what to do with himself. He turned his head and glanced over at Alika. What was the deal with her? Why were so many people after her? He shook his head and glanced her way one more time and thought, *'I wonder if there's a reward for her?'*

DEAN HAMID

CHAPTER EIGHT

Sabo and his partner Pete parked outside the front of a small ranch-style, one-story home. They got out and maneuvered around the other officers that had arrived first.

Sabo said, "Damn. I hope they didn't fuck nothing up." He reached into his jacket, pulled out some latex gloves and put them on.

There was a homicide detective he knew that came from the garage and spotted them. He walked towards them and said, "It's a bloody mess."

"A bloody mess." Sabo looked at Pete. "Been seeing a lot of that lately."

"Yeah, two Asian guys. One with his head bashed in. The other stabbed through the chest with a freaking chair leg… crazy." He shook his head and pointed towards the garage. "Back that way."

Sabo and Mike entered the garage. Mike surveyed the area and sniffed at the air. "There was a car here, fumes are still fresh."

"I smell it, too."

They moved slowly towards the doorway of the basement and eased their way down. Sabo noticed some chopped wood on a step below. He looked at the body and figured someone must have tripped him up, and he fell.

His partner kneeled over one of the bodies and looked closely. "He was hit upside the head pretty hard."

Sabo came over and looked at him. "That must have been the one that fell."

His partner looked up and said, "Someone was hiding."

"Probably the guy that was tied up in the chair." He looked over at the six by two wood beam and the pieces of rope that were cut, but still had knots. "The guy that did all this."

They walked over to the other guy.

"He put up a fight." Sabo kneeled and looked at his hands. "A big fight." He got up and looked at his sprawled-out body.

"So, you mean to tell me the guy that did him was big as he was."

Pete leaned over and looked at the stake driven into his chest and said, "Not really…just lucky."

Sabo smirked. "Yeah, *lucky*."

They took some notes and signaled for the criminal analysis team to come down and wrap things up. As they walked towards the car, Sabo looked over at Pete.

"Hmmm, Asian guys. Haven't heard anything about a war, but, something's up." He opened the door and slid into the car. "Need to make some calls."

****

Kim and Vong pulled into the parking lot of the Penobscot Building where they worked right around dusk. They waited patiently for security to make its rounds before they got out of the car and approached the building. Kim pointed to the side entrance, the door used for smokers. They congregated on the side of the building next to the door in a small alleyway. The smell of stale cigarettes and burnt butts permeated the air. Vong pulled at the door handle, and it was still open.

He looked awkwardly over at Kim and she said, "Probably because one of the security guards smoke."

Vong opened it cautiously and peeked in. There was no one, he waved at Kim to follow him as they crept inside. They found themselves in a stairway in the back side of the building, right behind the elevators. Vong peered his head out the stairway door and saw a security guard sitting at the desk and sighed.

"Damn," Kim said with a frown. "Hold up, I got an idea." She reached into her pocket for her cell phone. She dialed a number and peeked her head out of the door. The security guard's phone rang.

"Hello?"

Kim covered the speaker and spoke softly and sexy. "My car won't start. Can somebody give me a jump?"

They could see the guard as he stood and stretched his eyes out front, searching. "Where are you?"

"I'm over by the side of the building. It's getting late, the sun is going down...I'm scared!"

The guard rubbed his head and looked around for the rover, sucking his teeth. "Damn."

He stuffed his keys in his pocket and headed for the entrance. He opened the side glass door, then turned around and locked it shut.

"Good," Kim said as she put the phone away.

They dipped out of the door and hurriedly entered a waiting elevator, pressing floor six to Human Resources.

"How do we get in?" Vong asked.

Kim pulled a hairpin from her hair. "With a little luck, and YouTube."

Once they arrived at the floor and the elevator door opened, they dipped their head out. Not seeing anyone, they slowly tiptoed towards the entrance of the large door marked: *Human Resources*. Kim took the pin from her hair, stuck it into the keyhole, and jimmied it around and poking. She pulled it back out and wet it with her mouth, then stuck it back in and put her ear towards the lock. She twisted and the doorknob turned.

"Oh, shit," Vong gasped in awe.

She turned and gave him a wink. They crept slowly inside and made their way toward an office door, the supervisor's office. After opening the door and going inside, Vong surveyed the office, examining at least four computers. He spotted the one he was searching for. Then he pulled back a chair from the desk it was on and sat. Kim stayed by the door, watching out, while Vong turned on the computer and hacked into the mainframe. It took all of ten minutes or so before he was done. He inputted the mailroom's personnel files and as he scrolled down, he came across the name he was looking for: Nguyen, Lui.

"Got it." He scribbled the address down.

Kim leaned over his shoulder. "Do me a favor quick."

"What's up?"

"Look up Vien Phankham."

"Okay." He typed in the name, and it popped up quickly. He hadn't been dead for a little while, so they had yet to take it out of the database. He opened his file and scrolled around.

Kim stopped him and pointed. "There." Vong highlighted the area, and Kim read, "He was about to resign?" She read further. "But it says here he was being investigated for embezzlement."

"*Investigated?* They probably didn't have everything, and they offered him a resignation."

"Makes sense."

Vong inputted his name, accessing his personnel files. He went through a few folders, finding nothing but work stuff.

Kim spotted one that said, '*Alika.*' "Open that one up."

A screen flashed open, and some numbers popped up, then symbols and Asian writing They were the same symbols that were on Alika's back.

"What the hell!" Vong exclaimed.

Kim said, "Can you print that out?"

Vong looked around the office for a printer. He found it and accessed the line for it, then hit print. Sure enough, the printer came on and spat out the pages from the screen. Kim rushed over and grabbed them, then gave him the thumbs up once it was finished. He nodded and cut the computer off. Kim stuffed the papers in her shirt, and they snuck back out of the office. The elevator wasn't there, but Vong looked up and saw it coming.

"Did you press the elevator button yet?"
"No."
"It must be Security, we gotta go!"

They rushed for the stairway exit and opened the door leading their way downstairs. They quickly dipped out and made their way back to the car.

As they got inside, Kim noticed the security's Rover coming their way. "Got your ID?"

Vong fumbled around his jacket. "Here it is."

"When he comes through, just flash it at him."

He did, and the guard waved and kept it moving. They let out a sigh of relief. Vong cranked up the car and pulled off.

DEAN HAMID

CHAPTER NINE

Tran was sitting at his desk in his office ready to conduct business for the day when one of his servants tapped lightly at the door. "Sir."

Tran turned and answered, "Yes."

He pushed the phone he had in his hand toward him and said, "You have a call, sir…private line."

Tran frowned his eyebrows. "*Private line*? Wonder who that could be?" He got up from the table and retrieved the phone. "Tran."

"Hey, buddy."

"*Buddy,* what the hell?" He backed the phone up from his ear and turned towards his servant who immediately disappeared behind the door. "Who is this?"

"Sabo."

He snickered and walked toward the table where his food was and sat. "Sabo, what is it? I'm in the middle of something."

"Well, I won't be long then."

"Please." He picked up his fork and dug into the Thai-style omelet, Kai Jeow that sat in front of him.

"I'll get to the point." Sabo was in his office. He got up from his desk and closed the door, but not before looking both ways, then sat back down. "What's happening down in Madison Heights these days?"

Tran smiled then swallowed and said snidely, "Oh, you mean Chinatown. You know, the stuff you Americans like in a good old Asian community. Moo Goo Gai Pan…fireworks, laundry…all that." He snickered.

"No," Sabo replied dryly. "Murder…killings…dead bodies, that Madison Heights." There was abrupt silence. Sabo figured that would have gotten a rise out of him. "Wow, nothing slick…from you?"

"Sabo…" Tran put down his fork, wiped his mouth with the smock and leaned back, staring at the phone. He put it on speaker and tossed it on the table. "Those things you mentioned, I have no idea what you're talking about."

"Like I said, Murder…shootings…maybe, even a kidnapping."

"I have no idea what you're talking about…or implying." He tapped a glass with his spoon, and his servant popped his head in.

Tran pointed towards the half-eaten plate in front of him. The servant quickly came over and retrieved the dish. He stopped him then pointed towards the bar and nodded. The servant quickly put down the dish and ran over to the bar to pour a shot of Bourbon in a shot glass and brought it over to him. Tran picked up the glass, swallowed the liquor quickly, then nodded. The servant took all the dishes and the glass away and shut the door quickly behind him.

"Look, Detective Sabo, I am not affiliated with no criminal enterprises. Your department knows that, in Madison Heights or anywhere else. Maybe, you should ask the mayor about my character…"

"No…no, I don't have to do all that. I was just inquiring, that's all. Thought…we were friends." Sabo looked into the phone and grinned. Tran was too jumpy when he asked those questions, he knew something.

"We are, but I'm not familiar with what you ask me." He shook his head. "Not being rude but is there anything else? I have some pressing matters I must attend to."

"No, just asking."

"Okay, then, bye."

After he hung up with Sabo, Tran quickly dialed some numbers. "Hey, what's going on, Trang?"

"You find her yet?"

"We're close."

"Well, you need to get closer. I just got a call from your

nosy-ass cop friend. That means they're looking to make this into an inside Asian connection situation. Trying to connect this to me. We need to throw them off."

"I got you."

"Make sure of that!' He clicked the phone off and spun his chair around, facing the window in heavy thought. He had to put an end to this quickly. The Chut Suk across seas would ask questions about the little girl as well.

****

Kim paced the floor of the hotel room while Alika watched anime cartoons on the television. Every once and a while, she'd look up at her and shake her head, but now, she actually grew tired of it and spoke, "Be patient…"

Kim stopped briefly in her tracks and turned her way. "Trust me, I would love to be."

"There is nothing you can change. What will be, will be."

Kim twisted her head toward her. She couldn't believe the wisdom now coming out of this child's mouth. She thought about Malana. How she would also say things of that nature. Surely, Alika got it from her.

Kim sat next to her and said, "Thank you."

Alika put her arm around her, hugged her and whispered in her ear, "You are welcome."

Vong was outside in front of the hotel, waiting for his friend to arrive. As he stretched his neck up the block, he saw him coming his way. He greeted him in a gesture that was almost rehearsed, grabbing the hand and bumping the chest.

"Wassup, man!"

"What's happenin', family! I see you remembered."

"How could I forget, we had a blast in the mailroom."

"For sure…for sure."

Vong walked him to the hotel door where Kim had been staying. It was around the backside out of view. He knocked on the door. "It's me, Vong, I'm coming in!"

His friend tugged at him cautiously. "Yo man, everything cool?"

Vong smiled. "Yeah, it's good, just a friend of mine. Just wanted to make sure she's decent."

"Your girlfriend, huh?" He patted him on the back.

Vong was just about to lie his ass off when Kim swung open the door. Vong turned and said, "Kim, this is Lui, the guy I was telling you about."

Kim moved back slightly away from the door, looking him up and down. He stood at six feet or so and was slightly built. He had the Asian slanted eyes, but something was different about him. His eyes were wide and for her, very inviting. He had a fresh haircut that was tapered all the way around, even though it was more thick than stringy. He was handsome.

She held out her hand. "How are you, Lew?"

"Lui," he said as he walked through the door.

Kim pointed him over to the small sofa inside and sat. he looked around the place and saw Alika. He stared for a moment. She turned and waved at him. He waved back and looked over at Vong, who nodded his head toward her. Kim sat across from him on the bed and ruffled through her bag. She pulled out the book and handed it to him. Vong sat next to Lui and offered him a soft drink.

After flipping through the pages some, Lui looked up at them. "Yeah, this is old world Asian. A lot of stuff dealing with the Triads, and the Tongs. What does this have to do with you guys?"

Kim beckoned for Alika to come over toward them. She turned her around and pulled up her shirt, showing him the markings on her back.

Lui took a drink and gasped, almost spilling the soft drink all over himself. "What the hell!" Kim pulled down Alika's shirt and pulled her closer toward her. Lui looked over at Vong and said, "This…this is what you wanted to show me?" His face paled. "That is serious." He pointed towards Alika, put on his jacket and hurried toward the door. "Too deep for me!"

Vong tried to stop him. "What's wrong?"

He turned and looked at Alika. "You might want to ditch the kid."

Kim grabbed at him and spun him around. "No, that's not going to happen. Now, we called you over here to help us out. Apparently, you know something, at least tell us!"

Lui looked into Kim's eyes, seeing the deep sincerity in them. Alika was now frightened by his abrupt behavior.

He looked back over at Vong again and sighed, shaking his head. "Okay…okay." He stepped back towards the sofa and sat then picked up the book again. "This is some heavy Tong stuff."

"Tong?" Kim asked. "What's that?"

"That's equivalent to the mob in the United States, very hidden…secretive and above all…*dangerous*." He called Alika over and apologized to her, then asked her to turn around and pull up her shirt. "Those writings…they mean that she belongs to someone. And these markings here…" He pointed towards a series of long, twisted, branded lines. "…someone very high up, like a Chuk Sut."

DEAN HAMID

CHAPTER TEN

Her anxiety kicked in as Kim rose and paced the floor.

Lui could only look at Vong and say, "Hey, look, I'm sorry, but it's the truth." Vong picked up the book and flipped through pages as Lui continued, "That type of stuff in that book, where I'm from, is forbidden. I mean, you hear stories, but you hear and don't hear. Know what I mean?" Vong nodded his head in agreement. "The only way my mother… actually, my family got out of Laos was through a Chuk Sut. He made the arrangements, he paid the travel fees and everything."

Vong kind of twisted his head sideways and looked at him curiously. "He doesn't sound like a bad guy to me."

Lui humphed. "Yeah, but now my family owes him money.

"Okay…pay back the debt."

"For the rest of our lives…these guys are gangsters."

"So, why did you leave anyway?"

"Because we had to," he said solemnly.

Kim stopped and turned, facing him, sensing the apprehensiveness in his voice. Waiting to hear what he was going to say next.

"My mother had me…a bastard child. My father was an American in the Army over there. When his time was finished, he left."

Kim walked over slowly and asked, "So, at least you're with your family." She looked off. "Your mother."

Lui leaned back and looked up at her. "Yeah…right." He snided. "We were an embarrassment, we had to leave. The village looked at my mother like a whore."

"Sorry to hear that…"

"Naw…don't be." He waved it off. "We're better off in this country anyway. New identities…better lives."

"But what about the debt?"

"My mom…me…my brothers and sisters. We pay money every month or so. I mean…that's the life." He looked over at Alika. "Whoever her family is, was paid very well to put a Chuk Sut's mark on her."

"But what does it mean, does he own her or something?" Vong asked. "Maybe, he'd be willing to pay for her to get back to him, safely."

"Vong please!" Kim scolded. "You're always playing a hustle angle!"

"Hell, I got my ass kicked behind her! And, they wanted her that bad, they tortured me almost to death!"

Kim sighed, then turned back to Lui. "She can't be a slave, she's too young."

"Not really, Kim. But whatever those numbers mean…"

"Those were numbers?"

"Yeah, looks like they finished. Those brands though represent a signature of sorts. The child is valuable to someone high up."

Kim plopped down on the couch with her head in her hands. "So that's why they were killed."

Lui sat up, he looked at Kim then over at Alika. He turned towards Vong and said, "That's her?"

"Her, what do you mean?"

"The child, they're looking for her."

"Looking…who?"

Lui shook his head. "Check it, let me call someone who knows more about this than me."

"Who?" Kim said defensively. "We're already in enough shit!"

"No, he knows more than I do, trust me," Vong said.

"*Trust you*? You were ready to haul ass."

"I'm sorry about that. Just got spooked, now, let me call my uncle. He'll know what to do."

"Your uncle?" Vong said, "Who is he?"

"He's like an Asian-made man. He knows the Chuk Sut,

his name is Sen Hong."

Waiting around for Lui's uncle to arrive after he made the call, Kim figured now would be a good time to google a new hotel for them to stay in. She found one on the southwest side of Detroit. She pulled up one of her Visa card apps to pay for it, and her card was declined. Someone had hacked their way into her account. Whoever it was, was probably trying to get at Alika. Someone was on to her. It had to be someone that knew she had Alika. She paced the floor in thought, something dawned on her.

Her financial information attached to the cards she was using were tied into her job. It'd only been a couple of days maybe, a little over a week since she'd been in. She paused, remembering, she'd let HR know that she'd be gone for a while. She not being there shouldn't ring any bells. She was on leave, and she hadn't received any urgent texts from work. Someone had to be hacking her computer, or something.

"Damn, maybe one of those thugs that busted in the house…" A honking outside interrupted her thoughts.

She stopped and looked through the shades into the parking lot and spotted a dark-blue Crown Victoria slowly pulling into the lot.

She turned and called Vong over, "Hey, check this out, police!"

Vong got up and looked out. "Don't recognize…"

Lui had gotten up too and looked over his shoulder. "That's him."

He stepped to the door, and Kim stopped him. "Is everything cool?" She turned briefly and looked over at Alika. "Should she hide?"

He looked over at her also and said, "No, my uncle is alright." He opened the door and waved toward the car, stopping the dark-blue Sedan.

The Sedan turned around, then pulled up in front of the door of the hotel room. The passenger-side door opened, and a stocky, well-dressed Asian man stepped out, wearing a blue two-piece suit and a cream-colored shirt. He was clean cut and shaven, standing around six feet or so. He reached into his top pocket and pulled out some black Ray-Bans.

The driver's side door opened as well, and a much larger man stepped out of the vehicle. About as big as a Sumo wrestler, also Asian. He looked around and opened the long overcoat he wore, revealing the handle of a .45 tucked in his waist.

Sen Hong looked his way and nodded, walking towards the door. "Nephew!"

"Uncle Sen!" Lui greeted him and extended his hand, then stepped away from the doorway. "Come in."

Sen took another look at the driver and nodded once again. The driver nodded back and walked towards the side of the hotel room door, taking up a post. Sen stepped into the room. He still had on the dark shades, but you could tell he was staring by the slow way his head moved. Kim first, then Vong and finally, he focused on Alika. He walked towards her, and

Kim stepped in his way. "Nothing personal."

Sen stopped in his tracks, and a smile slowly appeared on his lips. "Of course."

She pointed him toward the sofa. He spotted the book on the side table. He took off his shades, slid them back into his pocket and looked over at Lui. "Interesting reading, I see."

Lui cut his eyes to the floor, frowning. He knew his uncle would disapprove of the book, and he would hear about it later.

Kim sat across from him and asked, "So, what's going on?"

"Going on, with what?"

"Okay, so, this is what we're doing?" She shook her head. "Well, for starters, why are they trying to kill Alika…Me? Why was her family killed? Why…"

"Whoa, okay… okay." He put up his hand toward her, stopping her. "I'll answer your questions." He looked over at Alika, asking, "Is the child okay?"

Kim looked back at her too and answered, "She's okay. Probably could use a better meal than those soups."

"That will be done." He looked up at her. "You are the woman that has been taking care of her."

"Yes." She reached out her hand. "Kim."

"Kim…Sen Hong."

"So, Mr. Hong." She looked over at Lui and asked, "What's going on?"

"Right now, a lot, I will not lie to you. But I will take care of everything from here, no more worries for you."

"You're going to take her?"

"But of course."

"Will she be safe?"

Sen Hong smiled, then leaned back. "I work for her family."

"Malana…Vien, I've never seen you before, and I knew her parents very, very well."

"No, her family in Laos. I've been ordered to bring her to her grandfather, Vinny Ta."

"Hold up, hold up." Kim shook her head. She was skeptical. "What about those marks on her back?"

Sen Hong glanced over at Lui and frowned. "You know about those…"

"Yes, I also know about this Chuk Sut thing. That she belongs to somebody?"

Sen smirked. "Not really, belong."

"Look." Kim got up and eased back toward Alika, reaching into her bag, faking like she was cuffing a gun, and said, "She's not going anywhere until I know exactly what the hell is going on. I mean that!"

Sen Hong didn't move, he just stared at her, then at the door. Kim followed his eyes, Lui's face had worry written all over. But, not for him, for Kim. He knew all his uncle had to do was call out, and his bodyguard would bust through the door. It would be a bad day for Kim.

He looked over at his uncle and said, "Please…"

He was surprised but very much relieved when he said, "Okay, this is what's going on. The child's mother, Malana, whom you so affectionately refer to, is Vinny Ta's daughter. Her father is a very wealthy man in Laos, the Chuk Sut."

"I know her family was very well off. I had no clue to this extent," Kim exclaimed.

"Her father did not want her to leave Laos for America. His only daughter, but she had gotten married, and it was no longer his choice. Vien received his blessing, after all, Vien was a smart, young man. Vinny Ta knew his family had dealings with the Hip Chong Tong, but he did not hold that against him. It was well known that Vien had no ties to that. So, Vinny Ta helped them go to the States, with his money, of course.

"Malana had made a few calls to him earlier about some strange behavior. Right about the time of the youngest child's birth, Alika. Vinny Ta rationalized it as a woman's emotional state during childbearing. She never disclosed anything he should have been alarmed about. He chalked it up to anxiety. But he still called me to look in on them from time to time. And of course, their affairs, I saw nothing wrong. Vien seemed like a good man, I watched as he finished his schooling… MBA. Malana finished school here as well, then followed tradition and started a family. I believe Vien had a pretty exclusive job."

"Yeah, he was the financial manager for the firm."

"Oh, so you worked with him?"

"Yeah also went to school with, Malana."

"Hmmm, interesting, I thought you looked familiar."

"Why do you say that?"

"Hell…that's probably why you've been so easy to track, I hear. But that's another story."

"You know, I was just thinking about that." Kim glanced over at Vong.

Catching her glance, Sen Hong continued, "Vien got mixed

up somehow or another with a guy named Tho Hoang Tran. He's a Dai Low here in America."

"Dai Low, what's that?"

"A boss...like a Godfather. He belongs to the notorious Hip Chong Tong."

"What does that have to do with, Vien?"

"Tran needed a man to move money for him. Someone he could trust. Someone who wouldn't bring up red flags. He had people on the inside...cops, but he probably couldn't manipulate them."

"I knew something wasn't right with them."

"You didn't go to them?"

"No, but..." She looked over her shoulder at Vong. "Vong said he was kidnapped by them. Vong!" she called out.

He rushed over by their side. "What's up?"

"Tell him about the cop situation...the kidnapping."

Vong looked at Sen and stuttered, but not out of fear. His eyes shifted towards the left like he was lying. "I don't know, Kim. I mean, I don't see how it will help matters."

"What did they look like?" Sen asked.

"They were Asian." He sighed. "They took me to this house, couldn't tell you where and tied me up." He lifted his shirt and showed him the burn marks on his chest. "They tortured me and everything."

"Hmmm, cops, you say? Did they show you a badge... or did you see one?"

"Naw, don't think they wanted me to know who they were. I mean..." He glanced over at Kim. "They shot up her apartment."

"*They*...I didn't hear anything about that, did you, Kim?"

"Well, I wasn't there, but I saw some creepy-looking dudes out of the window. So, I grabbed Alika and hauled ass. Vong stayed behind."

Sen Hong looked at over at Vong. "How did you get away?"

"Busted out, fought like hell, hauled ass and didn't look back."

Sen waited awhile, thinking he would divulge more. Like why shoot at him in the apartment? Must have been someone else there, and, how did he get to the house? He'd get with him later and get more into it. He was definitely holding something back.

"Okay, I'll check that out." He started to get up. "But, for now, we need to get you all to a safer place."

Kim stopped him. "Hold up, you never finished with the whole Tran thing."

Sen got up and peeked out the curtains then turned towards Kim. "Vien somehow got caught up with Tran, laundering money for the Hip Chong Tong. To what I now know, Tran was stealing money, and Vien found out. Tran made it seem like it was on him. With no other way to prove otherwise, Vien had no choice but to comply. Even made him pay for protection. What a scumbag, huh?"

"Why not tell them? The Hip Chong Tong themselves."

"His word against a Dai Low," Sen smirked. "No, that wouldn't work." He walked over to Alika and smiled, then kneeled beside her and rubbed her head playfully. "He did manage to get word to Vinny Ta, and they came up with a plan."

"A plan?"

"Yes." He called her over out of earshot from Lui and Vong. "The markings have a distinct meaning. They're part of a triad. There are three and when they're all put together, there's a code of sorts, mapping out where all the money Tran had stolen is hidden. That's why they want the little girl so bad."

"But... hold up," Kim interrupted. "Why didn't Vien just tell Vinny Ta everything?"

"Because there were also some people in his organization he couldn't trust." Sen looked at her steely-eyed. "People that were close around him. Vinny Ta figured it best that way to split up the numbers, or code. This way, if something ever happened to one of them…"

"And, Vien must have known he was marked."

"But, not his whole family." He stood and sighed. "We tried to get to the family to safety. But somehow, Tran found out and tried to torture them and find out the whereabouts of the markings. He already had one, he had no idea about the little girl until she came up missing."

"So, they know now."

"Yes, apparently, someone told them." He cut his eyes towards Vong.

He caught him, he walked towards them, saying, "Hey, I didn't say anything." He held up his hands and pleaded.

"Maybe so, but…unknowingly. Did they give you a drug?" Sen barked at him.

Vong's eyes widened. "Damn." He turned towards Kim, pleading, "If I did, I swear I didn't mean to."

Sen said, "That's okay, it is done."

Kim just shook her head disappointingly, looking at Vong, thinking about how much more he told them, and then asked Sen, "Okay, where do we go from here?"

"We get out of here." He walked to the door and opened it.

The bodyguard that stood out there came forward, and Sen whispered something to him. He nodded and walked to the car, opening the door. At that moment, another vehicle, also a four-door, dark sedan, sped into the parking lot. Sen turned and pushed everyone back inside the room and slammed the door shut. His bodyguard reached for his gun. The windows of the vehicle rolled down. A high-powered rifle and a shotgun were stuck out the windows, pointing their way, and fired at them. Sen dived behind the car. His bodyguard fired his gun, but he took two blasts in the chest and dropped.

The car stopped, and a short man in a black bandana covering his face stepped out, running behind the vehicle, looking for Sen. Sen managed to roll underneath the car and had stood on the other side. He came up behind the assailant, put him in a choke hold and snapped his neck. Sen looked up, and the other one opened the door, getting out. He made a break for the hotel room door. Lui had just opened it and ran out wanting to help, but Sen charged at him, backing him away from the door, and kicked it shut. He reached in his jacket and took out a gun.

"Leave!" He pointed to the back window. "I'll hold them off!"

"What about you!" Kim screamed back.

"Don't worry about me, just go!" He got up to his feet and ran towards the curtains, peeking out. Two more emerged from the car with guns. He looked over at Vong and said, "You know where to take them, now go, hurry!"

Kim threw some things into the bag and was already at the back window with Alika. She turned and looked back at Sen. He nodded at her, mouthing the words. "I'll catch up with you…be safe!"

CHAPTER ELEVEN

Tran stepped inside the back of the Maybach and directed his driver to Madison Heights. He needed to handle some business personally.

He reached into his pocket, pulled out his cell phone and dialed some numbers. "May-May, I'll be out for the rest of the day. Take the calls and schedule them for another time, okay?"

He sat back, checking out the lay of the land in Detroit, nodding his head and smiling. There was still a lot of money to be made there. If only he could just convince the City Council members to bulldoze the old dilapidated houses and subsequently rebuild. It would be advantageous for him to gain all that property for himself. From Madison Heights outward to the suburban areas. He'd settle them all with poverty-stricken Asians from his home to keep the property under his thumb.

This venture would also provide him with an array of tax loops he could exploit. At the same time, make him look good in front of the mayor and his own people. Who knows, maybe even make a run for the public office. After all, this was what America was all about. He pointed the driver to a three-story building that looked like an old firehouse. In fact, it was, but it was now Trang's office space.

The car pulled up front, and Tran looked out of a window on the third floor. The blinds opened briefly, then shut. He knew Trang was there, and more than likely, he probably wasn't expecting him. He got out of the car and walked inside. Trang's acknowledged his presence. He took the private elevator upstairs to Trang's office, and Trang opened the glass doors personally.

"Master Tran."

Tran was directed to a comfortable chair where his coat was taken, and he was brought a drink. Tran sat next to him and said, "Good to see you."

"Same here, Trang."

"It's rare to see you out in the community."

Tran crossed his legs, looking around at the high-dollar Asian sculpture: Buddha, Pagoda lanterns, and a six-foot dragon tucked off to the side. Either Trang's taste was getting exquisite, or he was ripping off the Asian shops that the tourists frequented…*ripping off the people sounded right.*

"It's good to see the people from home and see with my own eyes what's going on."

"Yes…it is."

"Ask questions." He took a sip of the Baijiu Chinese bourbon and turned towards Trang. "Hopefully, get answers." Trang had an idea why he was there, but now he knew for sure.

"Sure, Dai Low…sure. What do you want to know?"

"You tell me, Trang? I thought we would have this matter settled by now…the girl."

"Yeah…the girl." Trang got up and walked to the bar, pouring himself a stiff drink. "Well, apparently, we had them pinned down."

"Them?"

"You see, the little girl apparently is with this black chick. She's the one hiding her" He took a drink. "Probably the one who took her from the house in the first place."

"After you missed her."

"Yeah." Trang cut his eyes. "After she was missed." He sat back down. "We followed Sen Hong, he met with them. Of course, I sent my men over, but…"

"But?"

"But they got away."

"And, what about, Sen Hong?"

"I don't know yet, we have him held down."

"Yet, don't know? Got away, but…" Tran took another sip of his drink. "…these are not the words I want to hear, Trang. You said you had this, you told me not to worry. *So, now why am*

I worried, Trang?' He threw the glass at the wall, and it shattered, causing one of Trang's bodyguard to open the door. Tran gave him a stern look and he closed it immediately.

"We would have had them, but Sen Hong..."

"He should have been dead if he's not already." Tran got up. "You say you have him held down, let's go see!"

Trang got his coat, then opened the door and barked orders to his men. His car was cranked up, then several others pulled up behind. Trang got in the Maybach with Tran, and they all pulled off. His driver asked where they were going. Tran told Trang to tell him the hotel address.

****

Sen Hong raced towards the back window. He watched as Kim and the others ran off. He needed to give them more time to get out of sight. He raced towards the front door and peeked out the window through the curtains. Two others had gotten out of the car, and they were fast approaching the door. Sen Hong broke the glass and started shooting. They hit the ground and shot back. He jumped behind the bed for cover and fired more rounds out the window.

They were getting closer, he could hear them creeping up towards the door. Right now, he was running out of ammo. He eased back towards the window and fired the rest of his shots at the door. In the distance, he could hear the whine of the sirens of the police cars. They'd be there soon. He heard them outside shouting something like they wanted to burst through the door, but he knew they also heard the sirens getting closer. They argued about whether they should stay or go.

'*Good,*' Sen thought, that was all he needed, a little hesitation.

He jumped through the back window and hid beneath an old wooden fence in the alleyway. It sounded like they were making their way toward the back. But no one came, and he sure as hell didn't want to wait around for anyone either. He made his escape.

****

Sabo had gotten the call in his office first. Shots fired inside an old hotel over on the Southwest side. He was about to ignore it and send someone else until he heard the description, *Asians*. He had a good hunch that this had something to do with what he was looking into. He called his partner, they got in a car making their way towards the Southwest side of Detroit.

****

Tran's car pulled up across from the hotel where the scene was escalating. Police cars pulled up, and the manager was already out front pointing and yelling something in an Indian dialect they couldn't understand, adding to the chaos. It wasn't him they were called in to quell the havoc. It was the shots coming from the back end of the hotel.

Tran had Trang order his men to park, get out and blend in with the crowd that had gathered, and to keep their ears and eyes open. The police cars were now pulling in towards the back end of the hotel, with weapons drawn as they jumped out of their cars. The three men trying to get at Sen earlier, now had their attention drawn toward them. One of them made the mistake of firing a few shots, and all hell broke loose.

He tried to run and make a break for the back side of the building, but his plans were thwarted by a few cars that had already pulled around the back in the alleyway. He fired shots at them, and they returned fire, striking him and bringing him down. The other two ducked behind a car taking cover. One pointed toward the door and ran toward it. He kicked at it, and it busted open. He dipped inside, and the other one tried to do the same but was caught in the crossfire between him and the police.

They dropped him right in front of the door. Tran watched keenly as it all transpired.

He asked Trang, "Your men, I assume?"

"Yeah," Tang replied as he too watched his men go down one by one in the carnage. "Shame, good men too."

"Of course, they had no ID or anything that could identify who they were…or draw them to me."

"No, of course not." He watched as the other police officers moved toward the door of the hotel room. "He's trapped."

"Think he'll give up?"

"He shouldn't…" Trang glanced over, and he stepped out of the room with his hands up. The police tackled him to the ground, handcuffing him.

"Damn, doesn't look good. I may have to call my people and get him to shut up, permanently."

Trang looked over at one of his men, put up his hand and said to Tran, "No need."

Sabo and his partner pulled up to the scene in time to watch the police as they wrestled the assailant to the ground, handcuffing him.

"They got one," he said, "Good… we need to question him."

His partner tapped him on the arm. "Hey, look over there, isn't that Tran's car?"

Sabo looked. "Hell yeah, and that's that crony Trang in the car with him. What do you know? A known Asian mobster." He opened the car door and turned towards Tran. "Hey, Pete, go check out the perp. I want to have a quick word with, Tran. Or, the so-called good man of the people."

His partner nodded and stepped through the crowd that had gathered towards the hotel. Sabo walked over to the car and tapped on the window.

The window came down and Tran said, "Detective Sabo,

good to see you." He peered behind him. "Bad situation there, glad your people are handling it."

Sabo leaned inside the window of the car and turned toward the hotel. "Yeah, that's what we do. He, uh, looks Asian." He peeked into the car and looked over at Trang. "Familiar with them?"

Trang smirked. "No, sir, just another Asian. He was probably delivering the laundry, and maybe the manager didn't like the sheets." Tran laughed lightly.

"Smart ass, huh? Maybe," Sabo said. "Or, maybe the manager couldn't afford to pay him, so he shot the place up. He and his boys. How about that one, Trang? Sound familiar, huh?"

Trang frowned and spat, "What is it you want, Sabo?"

"Just thought it was strange seeing you two together, that's all," Sabo said, looking over at Tran. "But, I'm sure it's a community matter you guys are discussing, huh, Mr. Tran?"

"Yeah, community matter. That's it, smart cop, Sabo."

"If I find out any of you had something to do…" A shot was fired, and Sabo ducked and turned around.

Someone had stepped from the crowd and assassinated the gunman they had in cuffs. When the cops turned to draw on whoever it was, he ducked into the crowd. They gave chase, but it was useless, he'd disappeared.

Sabo turned around and mean mugged Tran, then hightailed it toward the scene. Tran looked over at Trang and said, "Good man."

"He may need to lay low for a while, though."

Tran reached into his pocket and took out a pen to scribble an address. "Here, tell him to go there, he'll be taken care of."

Trang took the number and smiled. Tran rolled up the windows, telling his driver to go. Sabo made it over, and the guy was dead, shot through the head. He looked over with disdain as Tran's car pulled off. It was definitely Trang's M.O.

He followed his partner close to the hotel room. They

stepped through cautiously, looking around. The police had already cleared it for any other shooters and were coming back out. Sabo walked toward the back window which was wide open.

He looked down at the body of one of the shooters that was sprawled out. "Looks like he was trying to get out through here."

His partner looked out. "Maybe, behind a few others."

Sabo checked the drawers and bathroom. "Definitely there were others here."

An officer rushed through the door. "Detective Sabo." He had a hotel ledger in his hand. "The room was paid for with a credit card registered to a company account."

"Was there a name on it?"

"No, just a location code…probably tracking, or billing."

"Okay." He took the ledger and looked at it, then gave it to his partner. "Tracking this lead will be easy enough."

"Probably the girl."

"More than likely."

His partner picked up the book Kim had left behind during the rush. "What's this?"

Sabo came over and looked through it. "Evidence."

DEAN HAMID

CHAPTER TWELVE

Lui pointed them towards Warren where he'd make a call and have someone pick them up once nightfall came. Until then, they hid in an abandoned house on John R. Kim took the time to ruffle through her bag, looking for a heavier shirt to put on Alika. It was getting much cooler now.

"It's getting cold out, and I don't even have a jacket for her!" Kim stated.

Lui moved over toward her, comforting her. "Don't worry, when we get to where we're going, there will be better clothes for her."

"And. hopefully a hot meal, she hasn't eaten since this morning…"

"Don't worry." Lui rubbed her shoulders, and Kim seemed to fall back into his caress, easing her anxiety.

Vong looked over, watching them, he was jealous. "Why is Kim giving affection to him and not me?" He wondered silently. His blood boiled every time Lui rubbed her arms. "Look at that double-crossing bastard!" He'd had enough. "You know what?" He stepped toward them. "Why the fuck are we running?"

Lui and Kim turned his way. "What do you mean?" Kim asked.

"I mean, we're not the one they want." He pointed towards Alika. "She is…why not just give them the kid?"

Kim shook her head, she couldn't believe what she was hearing from Vong. "What are you saying, Vong?"

"Kim, I've been going through all this shit!" He turned away, peeking out the window. "Getting beat up…hiding! But, for what!" He turned around. "I didn't sign up for this shit."

Lui stepped between them. "What do you suppose we do?"

Vong was visibly shaken from all that had happened. He

leaned against the wall, trying to calm himself. He took a few deep breaths, then said, "Gangsters…shootouts…this is way too much for me." He looked over at Kim. "You're a friend and all, but I've had enough."

"But…"

"No buts, Kim, I put my own mother at risk, and who knows who else. These guys are dangerous, Kim. You should have gone to the police with the child when you had the chance, and even now…you still can." He looked at Lui. "You may want to consider it." He walked toward the door and opened it. "They killed her whole family. What do you think they'd do to me…*us*? I'm tired of it." He opened the front door, hesitated, and looked back around at Lui. "You staying?"

"Of course!" he spat. "Of course, I gave my uncle my word!"

"Well, I didn't." He slammed the door behind him as he left.

Kim started crying, and Lui rushed over to her. "Don't cry, I got you. I'm going to make a call my cousin will pick us up and take you both somewhere safe. I promise."

"But we don't even know if Mr. Sen made it out of the hotel room alive."

"Knowing my uncle…I'm sure he did." But, even as Lui said that he was unsure of it.

He was also worried for Kim as well as himself. He looked down at her wiping the tears from her eyes, and Kim looked up at him. She kissed him, and he responded by kissing her back. She pulled him close to her, feeling the hardness of his body as she did. Lui tenderly caressed her hair and stroked her back in a careful and gentle manner.

Kim pushed him away tenderly. "Alika… is watching."

Lui looked over, and Alika was indeed watching. She walked over and stared upward at them. Her pretty, bright eyes held wells of tears ready to burst.

"Damn," Kim mumbled, she'd made a bad move. "How

could she trust her now?" But, Alika hugged her and reached out to hug Lui too.

****

Vong walked up I-75 toward a pay phone. He figured he'd call his mother and catch a cab over there. As he thought about the whole situation, he just simply concluded it wasn't worth it. He stopped for a second. What the hell was he thinking? The child was worth money. Trang's people wanted her, and that guy Vinny Ta, The Chuk Sut. He knew or at least had an idea where Lui was taking them. He could always get back in touch with them if he needed to. Kim trusted him. So, why not sell that information to the highest bidder? Why should he lose?

He turned and looked up the highway toward Madison Heights. A long walk granted, but worth it. He turned around in that direction, and in his mind, made plans on how he would negotiate the matter and who he'd go to first. Vong walked as far as he could. Tired and hungry, he was second-guessing his reasons for leaving Kim and Lui in the first place.

Maybe he was a little too rash, quick with his judgment. The wind picked up, and he wrapped his hands around himself trying to stay warm.

"To hell with it," he told himself.

The next pay phone he saw, he would call his mother and have her send him a cab. Then he'd go home where it was warm and safe. Up ahead, he spotted Ajax Drive and knew he was close. He could smell some of the lo mein that permeated the air, making his stomach grumble. He walked a little further and saw what he was looking for. A pay phone inside a local store, but across the street from it was the old fire station set up as Trang's headquarters.

He hesitated and looked both ways, thinking about earlier, as his mind started rambling. Those thoughts that still bothered his conscience. He needed to decide, but all he could think about was Kim in Lui's arms. He crossed the street, heading toward the firehouse. Trang's men were outside. One of them spotted him and told him to stop while the others looked him over.

Vong yelled out to them, "Please, tell Mr. Trang…"

A car pulled up directly in front of him, screeching to a stop. The door swung open and Vong's eyes widened as he saw who it was.

"I sort of figured you'd sell them out, get in!" It was Sen Hong.

Vong looked over at Trang's men as they moved closer toward him, reaching into their coats, more than likely for guns. He could run toward them yelling that Sen Hong was in the car.

Sen pulled out a gun and pointed it towards him. "Get in now, I'm not going to tell you again!"

Vong made his decision and got in the car. It sped off, and Sen turned toward him. "I'm not going to kill you…even though I should."

"I…I…I was just going to…" Vong stammered.

"Going to tell where my nephew is hiding." Sen pointed the driver toward the neighborhood where his nephew was hiding and looked back over at Vong. "Don't worry, you'll have your chance to redeem yourself…trust me."

Sen pulled up in the driveway of the old beat-up house. He'd made some calls, and he was led there, more than likely from a call made by Lui earlier. Vong already knew where it was but didn't bother to divulge any information. He ordered Vong out of the car, and they approached the door.

Lui swung it open. "Uncle, you're safe!" He glanced over at Vong. "What are you doing with him? He left us, thought he was going home, or something."

Sen shoved him through the door. "Actually, he did, just not his."

Kim stepped from out back and when she saw Vong, she sneered. "Oh, you came back."

"No, not exactly," Sen said, "Now, get your things, and let's get out of here."

"Where are we going?" Vong asked.

Sen got up in his face and spat, "Oh no, not this time. Trust me, you'll see when we get there." Lui snuck up behind him and knocked him out cold.

Sen pointed Kim and Alika to the car while he helped Lui pick up Vong, and they dragged him to the car. Sen opened the trunk and tossed him in.

"Will he be alright?" Kim asked.

"He will, I just don't want him to see where we're going."

"You think he'd tell?"

Sen got in the car and cranked up. "Where do you think he was going when I got up with him?"

Kim gasped. "Dirty mutha…" Alika punched her leg and frowned. "Oh… okay, you know what I mean."

Lui and Sen laughed as the car pulled down the driveway headed toward Highway 75. They pulled in an alleyway behind a restaurant. Sen opened the door, telling them they'd arrived.

"Where?" Kim asked.

He replied, "A safe place."

She grabbed the bags, and Sen pointed them toward the back door, instructing them to knock. The door quickly opened, and two men came out. Both dressed in white restaurant worker coveralls. Sen called them over as he opened the trunk. He barked more orders, and they immediately pulled Vong out. They picked him up and walked toward the door. Sen nodded for Kim to follow them. The men turned toward a door directly to their left and opened it. Kim peeked in, and there was a staircase leading down, perhaps into a basement. She followed them, but Sen came through the door behind her and guided her forward, shutting the door behind the two men carrying Vong's body down the stairs.

It was a large kitchen the ambiance was busy and there was lots of food being prepared. The air smelled of boiled vegetables, noodles, garlic, and onions. She peeked at one of the long, steel prep tables and spotted chopped-up bell peppers, bean sprouts, mushrooms, and cut-up chicken. She smelled the sautéed soy sauce in the air seasoned with ginger. Alika's eyes beamed as she looked around at the different delicacies. Kim's stomach grumbled, and Lui giggled.

Sen looked at one of the older men who appeared to be in charge and said something to him in Asian. He looked over at Kim and Alika and smiled, telling them to come with him. He led them out front to the restaurant. Beautiful was all Kim's mind could muster. She marveled at the brilliance of the decor.

The walls were caramel-oak with reflective lighting coming from the top. The tables were covered with white linen accompanied by padded chairs. Mirrors intermittently lined across the walls. In the middle of the floor was a large Bonsai plant that had a water mote around it with live goldfish. Toward the front was a similar decoration, but it was a large, sprouting fountain with a crystal chandelier placed above it.

She glanced to her right, and there was a full bar off to the side with dim inwardly set lights that made the crystal glass glimmer, and bar stools with the same material as the cushions on the floor. It was uniquely beautiful.

"Is this Sen's?" Kim asked.

Lui replied, "It belongs to our family."

"Wow."

She and Alika were escorted to a table with dishes immediately brought to them. The first of many dishes to be placed out for them. Kim and Alika turned toward Sen, and he nodded.

"Go ahead…eat, as much as you like. I'll have some fresh clothes brought to you."

Kim started to say something but just shook it off. Sen knew what it was already. He smiled as he watched Kim and Alika dive into their plates.

Lui asked Sen, "Will they be alright here?"

Sen smiled. "I'm sure." He put his arm around Lui and said, "You watch over them, I have to get in touch…"

"With Vinny Ta."

"Yes, Vinny Ta…arrangements for the child has to be made to leave and go to him."

"What about the girl, Kim?"

"Well, nephew, I see the way you watch her. That's on you."

Lui turned and looked Kim's way. "On me…right."

DEAN HAMID

CHAPTER THIRTEEN

Sabo sat in his office going over files, reports, and everything he knew thus far. He'd already drunk three cups of coffee and was working on a fourth. It was getting late and the hustle and bustle of the office lightened up some. Most of the other detectives were on their way home for the day.

His partner Pete came in. "C'mon, Sabo, it's getting late. Let's call it a day." He looked around at the paperwork scattered about his desk. "It'll be here tomorrow, let's get a drink."

Sabo looked up and nodded. "Okay, sounds good but hold up…"

"Wha…"

"Just check this out, Pete, C'mon, give me…" He looked around his desk and picked up a report. "…a minute." He pointed him toward a seat. "Have a seat, hear me out."

Pete sighed and sat. "Okay."

Sabo kicked his feet off his desk and leaned forward. "This is what we got so far…a whole family murdered."

"Asian."

"Yeah, Asian, all murdered except a child. Now, did they miss the child…did the child get away?"

"The girl."

"The girl, okay, let's deal with that. We know who she is. Hell, she really wasn't trying to keep it secret, to what we know, or we're assuming she had nothing to do with the murders, period."

"I can see that."

"So then, why is she involved?"

Intrigued, Pete leaned forward, pondering on the direction

Sabo was taking him. "Well, we know she worked with the little girl's father. We know she went to school with the mother."

"Right, so, why didn't, and still doesn't she come to us? The police."

"Hmmm." Pete leaned back. "Good point, why then?"

"Only way I see it is because she was scared, and still is." Sabo peered up, looking around. "Scared of someone in here."

"Makes sense."

"Okay, now, check this out." Sabo picked up some more paperwork and flipped through it. "We questioned numerous Asians in the close-knit community, and no one knows nothing."

"Or, they're just not talking."

"Business owners, the old-timers, even the gangs… nothing!"

"Being quiet for a reason, but what?"

"So, we can assume it's bigger than them. So, who is bigger than them?" One of those *I think I got it* grins slowly appeared on his face.

"Trang?"

"Trang, naw, at the end of the day, he's just a two-bit thug…much bigger."

"Tran?"

"At least, it's got to be. He's the puppet master. Then, when we mention something to him, of all people, he acts like he doesn't know shit. Impossible, he's damn near the fucking mayor of the Asian population in this city."

"Yeah…so far, you're making sense."

"All of it does, Pete." Sabo got up and walked to the coatrack, grabbed his jacket and put it on. "Too much sense."

****

Sen Hong walked through the kitchen toward the door that led down into the basement. He opened it and waved one of his men over.

"Watch the door, make sure no one comes through." He looked over at the older man in charge and pointed toward the front. "Oh, yeah, make sure they have clean clothes."

He gave him the thumbs up and walked down the stairs. When he reached the bottom step, he glanced over to the right. Two men stood guard, right next to them was a chair tied to a metal pole. In the chair sat Vong, tied down. Sen signaled for them to step away and grabbed a seat in front of Vong.

He shook his head, snickered and leaned into him. "Here we go again." Vong looked him in the eyes and tried cussing him out. It would have had some effect, but his mouth was gagged. So, Sen just laughed at him. "The last time I snatched you up, you got away. I blame that on Trang. I told him to watch you." He leaned back and watched as Vong's eyes widened at the shock of what he was saying. "Oh, yeah, Trang and I are partners."

He reached into his pocket and pulled out a cigarette. "We've been partners for a while too. You see, we plan on taking down not only Tran but Vinny Ta as well. We're going to use their own men, and even…greed, to take each other down. Make it seem like the Hip Chong Tong and Vinny Ta are warring with each other, but in fact, it's just us pulling the strings. Trang has control over Tran and his men. I have control over Vinny Ta and his men. And they do whatever we tell them. So, eventually, they will beg us to end it and Detroit as well. And, of course, we'd oblige, looking almost like… hmmm, heroes."

Vong wriggled about in the chair, and Sen reached over for his gag. "No one can hear you that will help you. So, the yelling truly would be in vain." He snatched it off.

Vong spat out lint balls that had gathered in his mouth and yelled, "You sick bastard!"

"Me…why would you say that? After all, wasn't it you that was going to tell Trang where the girl was?"

Vong looked away, Sen was right.

"Yes, you see, you get it now, but you just don't know how to put it together."

"I just wanted to bait her, not give the girl up!"

"But, you did it all for money. Money they would have never paid you. They would have killed you first. And yes, the little girl is worth a lot of money. Her father Vien funneled millions into an account, then had enough sense to split up the codes for the account. He passed them out, each a third, passed them out to each other's enemies. They would have to kill each other to acquire them…genius."

"But, the girl. Why is she still alive now? You know the numbers are tattooed on her back!"

"Because not only was the code numerical, it was also verbal. The little girl knows the language."

"The language?"

"An old-world dialect he taught her personally. The only one is the world, except for three other people."

"Who!"

"Tran, and of course, Vinny Ta!"

"So, you want to put Vinny Ta against the Tong and have them kill each other off?"

"And that would leave me… and Trang, the only two standing. Trang would easily slide into his role as Dai Low of the Hip Chong Tong, and I would become the Chuk Sut… easily."

"You dirty, double-crossing…"

"But yes, of course." He stuffed the gag back into his mouth. "One thing, though…" He got up from the chair and turned to leave. "I'm really thinking of what to do with you. Killing you would be such a waste because you're a piece of shit yourself. And I can use a man like you." He signaled his men back over and went up the stairs, laughing.

Sen Hong went upstairs, back through the kitchen and into his office, closing the door behind him. The restaurant belonged to him. Lao Blue Lagoon, a gift from Vinny Ta. Sen Hong set up all his family members there, including Lui's family.

Many were in Vinny Ta's pocket for quite a while, and he knew the majority of them would be for the rest of their lives. He and his family resented that. He also resented what Tran represented as well. At first, he was big with his plan to build up an Asian presence in Detroit and subsequently purchased a lot of the property. Abandoned homes, businesses, warehouses rebuilt and gave Detroit a Northern Asian feel.

It would be a paradise for many Asian refugees. But Tran grew corrupt, partnering with the Hip Chong Tong and stealing money. Sen made the call to put Vien in the loop, figuring it would secure some easy finances. He could go on his own, away from the corruption, but he was double-crossed. Then, the murder of Vien's family. He didn't feel that was necessary, and it was all he could take.

Trang didn't approve of the action either. It would have been worth it to him to just hide the family, but Tran wouldn't have it. He hired a gang from the Hip Chong Tong on the low to do the dirty work. It was a miracle Alika got away, but even a bigger miracle that she ran right into Sen Hong's arms. The cards were playing in his favor.

He sat at his desk and picked up the phone. "Hello, let me speak to *Gung-Gung Ta*."

"He's in the garden, I will get him."

"I will wait."

Sen put the phone on speaker and sat back, replaying the story he would tell the elder, the *Gung-Gung,*' Vinny Ta, over and over in his head. After hearing a few murmurs in the background, the phone was picked up on the other end.

"Sen."

"Master Vinny Ta."

"Do you have her?"

"Yes, she's here with me now."

"Good...good," Vinny Ta spat a few words in Chinese, more than likely for someone to bring him a chair. "Hold on, Sen." He was also brought a ledger and he opened it to reveal dates. He pulled on his long, white beard, analyzed a few entries, and spoke back into the phone. "Clearly, Tran has been stealing money. I need to divulge the truth to his Chuk Sut...his grandfather, but I will need solid proof. This type of foolishness could make war. The girl, she must be brought to me soon!"

Sen opened a drawer in his desk, pulled out a flask, opened it, and said, "Arrangements are being made." He took a sip.

"Good, Sen. The only way to make things right is to give back the money Tran stole."

"But will Tran admit he was behind everything or blame it solely on Vien."

"Good point, that's why I want the girl with me. To not only have access to the money but to keep her safe."

"But once she divulges what's needed from her, will she be needed anymore?"

Vinny Ta laughed, then coughed hoarsely. He knew he didn't have much time, and soon, he would have to appoint a successor. Right now, he had no son. Just daughters, and plenty of sons-in-law he couldn't trust with a task of that magnitude. He needed a trustworthy individual.

Sen Hong thought maybe it would be him, but Vinny Ta knew differently. He knew of his dealings. He also knew he was holding back something, but right now, his focus was on Alika. Securing the money and the sacred language he had entrusted with her father for the purpose of the code. That was something Sen didn't know about.

"She will be forever...needed."

Sen frowned his dark, bushy eyebrows. "What do you mean, Vinny Ta?" he asked.

"You'll know soon." He called out to someone and a woman came over. "Tell my daughter here when you are planning to bring the child."

He was about to hang up, and Sen said, "Wait!"

"Wait?"

"Yes, it will be difficult to secure a plane for her in the States. It would be better if one came in from over there. Your private jet."

"From here?"

"Yes, Gung-Gung, and to be honest, my best advice. You should be here to secure her."

"Why me?"

"It will show power. The people here will see that and show their respect."

"Hmmm, I see," he said. "Okay, one week. Can you secure the child for one week?"

"Yes."

"Good, the matter is settled. I will speak to you later in the week."

"Yes, sir."

His daughter got on the phone. "I will call and let you know when and where we will be coming in."

"Maybe you should use…"

"I said I will call you and let you know. Bye."

The phone clicked off in his ear, and he leaned back. Still pondering what he meant about the girl, were there more secrets? Tran probably knew more than what he was leading on. He would need to get in touch with Trang and find out. Until then, Kim and Alika would stay there with him.

Lui walked over to the table where Kim and Alika were and sat, amused at the way they gulped down their food. "You two are a sight to see."

Kim laughed softly and said, "If you've been through what we've been through lately."

Alika giggled, and Lui looked over at her. "No more Ramen noodles, huh?" She shook her head and continued eating.

Kim pushed away her plate and wiped her mouth. "What

about you, aren't you hungry?"

"I'll grab a bite later." He pointed to the kitchen. "It's not like there won't be any later."

Kim smiled. "Such a big place. Your family's?"

"Actually, it was given to, Uncle Sen."

"Given…a place this big?"

"By Vinny Ta, Uncle Sen's family works for his family in Laos, and Sen was sent here." He looked around and beamed at the place. "I heard there were other reasons as well."

"Like what?" Kim asked.

"Well." He leaned in closer toward her. "I heard he was sent to keep an eye on Tran. His Chuk Sut didn't trust him. They're trying to get the money that was…" He glanced over at Alika, then whispered, "…stolen."

"Yeah, that it was."

Alika pushed away her plate and rubbed her stomach. "Hong noa."

"Hong…what?" Kim gasped.

Lui got up from the table and reached for her and said to Kim, "She's saying…bathroom." He called out toward the kitchen, a slim, slightly older woman came out, grabbed her by the hand and escorted her away. Kim was ready to pounce like a protective lioness, but Lui put up his hand. "She's perfectly safe, trust me." Lui watched and said, "You're safe as well."

Sen peeked from out back and called Lui over, "Be right back."

When Lui approached him and Sen said, "Let them know they will be staying here for a while."

"A while?"

"Not long, until we secure everything for the little girl to leave."

"Okay, Uncle."

Lui came back over toward Kim and said, "My uncle says you can stay."

"Stay?"

"Well, until the girl leaves."

"Where is she going?"

"Back to Laos, to Vinny Ta, where she would be safe."

"Is she not safe here?" Kim asked as she looked around.

"Of course, but her grandfather wants her to come to him."

"I understand, that is her only family." She sighed.

Lui pointed Kim toward the bar, they walked over and sat. He called over a shapely Asian woman. "Can I help you, sir?"

"Yes, Gin and Tonic and…"

He turned to Kim, and she said, "I'll have the same."

After a short while, the drinks arrived, Lui asked, "So, what's next for you?"

"Hell." Kim shrugged her shoulders. "Hopefully work, if that's even safe for me these days."

"I'm sure my Uncle will take care of things for you."

"Well, …we'll see."

"What I meant was." He took a swig. "Home…family…maybe… even a boyfriend?"

Kim smiled. "The only family I have is my father. And no, I have no one."

"That's sad."

"What, just me having only my father?"

Lui said, "No, No, I didn't mean that."

Kim laughed and moved closer toward him. "Then… what did you mean?"

Lui got closer as well and said softly to her, "A boyfriend."

Alika came back from the bathroom to the front of the restaurant, and Kim said, "Hold up, Lui, there's Alika." They stood and went over toward her. "You okay, sweetie?"

Alika smiled and nodded her head. Lui whispered to Kim, "Doesn't talk much…"

"She's been through a lot, I was like that as a kid."

"Someone tried to kidnap you?"

"No, my dad was abusive."

"Wow." Lui looked over at her. "He hit you?"

"Worse, it seems like, it was verbal, I became withdrawn. Had anxiety attacks growing up." She smiled at Alika. "Actually, it was her mother who helped me adjust. Spiritually... mentally." She looked off to conceal the anguish she felt. "I do miss her."

Lui reached out and held her hand. She smiled and squeezed his. Alika stretched and yawned. "Tired, huh, sweetheart?" She nodded again.

Lui quickly stepped into the back, and the same woman who led Alika to the bathroom came back out with him. "Kim. This is Changying, my cousin, she's going to show us to our rooms."

Kim looked around. "There are rooms in here too?"

"Actually... The whole building is four stories. We live up top in the apartments."

"Okay...do you have your own place then?"

They fell in behind Changying as she led the way to a stairway. "I do when I'm here."

"When you're here? I don't understand."

"I actually have my own place *per se.*" He pointed out of a window on a ledge. "Over there, not much, but it's my own. For privacy...ya know."

"Oh, don't I know."

They reached the top floor and opened the door. There were two long hallways with doors to different apartments. Changying walked toward the end of the hallway and stopped in front of a door. She took out some keys then handed them to Kim.

"This is where you stay." She looked down at Alika. "With the little girl." Changying walked into the two-bedroom space and pointed to the clothing laid out on the sofa. "Clothes for you and her."

"Oh, thank you."

"You are welcome." She pointed to the bathroom.

"Hygiene items too."

Kim thanked her again and by that time, Alika laid on the sofa and not too much longer, she was fast asleep. Kim and Lui tiptoed toward the door.

"I guess I'll see you...later?" Kim grabbed his hand and pulled him closer, watching as Changying stepped into the stairway. "Where are you staying?" Lui pointed toward another door not too far away.

"There?" Kim looked back. "Will she be alright...here alone?"

"Yeah, but I don't think it's a good idea to leave her. You know...alone."

"You're right." Kim pulled him in and closed the door behind him. She peered into the bedroom. "I just don't want to be by myself. So much has happened."

"I understand."

They walked inside the bedroom, and Lui sat on the side of the bed. Kim sat across from him, stretching out. "This feels so good."

Lui looked over. "I bet it does."

"It would feel...a lot better..." She playfully grabbed his arm and pulled him closer to her. Putting up no resistance, Lui gently crawled on top of her and kissed her. Kim caressed his shoulders. Lui slowly grinded himself into her. His dick growing hard as he did. Kim responded by moaning passionately in his ear. Meeting him, grind for grind.

Lui kissed her neck, and she cooed. She pushed him off her slightly and leaned up. As she did, she slid up her shirt, letting Lui eyeball her beautiful, cocoa-brown skin. She unfastened her bra, revealing her full, plump breasts, rising and falling seductively as she breathed in and out. The dark-chocolate areola framed her thick nipples as they got hard.

Lui climbed off the bed and stood over her, taking off his shirt as well. Kim admired his ripped, lean-muscled, smooth, olive skin. As she stared, she noticed a large tattoo across his bicep of a dragon.

"What's that?"

"This one on my arm is a Shenlong, it represents spirituality. When I was young, in Laos, I was part of an uh, what you would call, a gang."

"A gang...you?"

"I was lost, always in trouble...cutting school. I needed direction and that's where I tried finding it."

Kim leaned up, getting closer to him, and asked, "So, what happened?"

"My older cousin introduced me to Uncle Sen. He helped my family and my mother get out of the slums. Then, we came here to America. Away from the *'gangs.'*"

"Deep..."

"Uncle Sen tells me I come from a good family, but he won't say who they are. I don't know, my mother won't say either. She just says she embarrassed them, and they put her out on the street. All of us...the whole family."

"Wow, you ever wonder what happened?"

"I just leave it alone and do me. My life is different now."

She pulled him closer to her, opening his pants and pulling them down. She leaned down, hugging his tight ass, and pulled down his boxers. She kissed the tip of his dick. Lui's head bobbed backward as his dick started to rise. Kim looked up at him, then grabbed hold of his dick and engulfed it in her mouth, pulling him in and slobbing the tip in her mouth. Lui moaned and reached for the back of her head, matching her back and forth in her mouth. Kim finally let up, he was rock hard, and his veins were throbbing.

She crawled back on the bed and unfastened her pants. Lui reached over to joyfully help her. As he slid them off, he couldn't help but admire Kim's shapely body. She pulled off her panties and threw them on the floor, then smiled, giving him the look. Her pussy had a small patch of curled brown hair, exposing a budding red clit. Backing up some more on the bed, she opened her legs invitingly.

Lui didn't need any more of an invite, and he got on top of her, kissed her lips and neck, then moved down to her breast. He sucked her nipples like a thirsty child. She moaned and grabbed the nape of his neck, pulling him down closer. She was soaking wet and dripping, so she opened wider and could feel his rock-hard dick rub and throb against her inner thighs. She grabbed it, guided it into her and moaned as the heat of his dick entered her now wet pussy. He thrust, and it seemed to fill her up, and he continued to stroke.

She had never felt this level of passion, or pleasure before. He continued kissing her and stroking, hitting every corner. Slow, then fast, rhythmically. He moaned, she moaned, and they sweated. The heat poured off their body like steam.

Kim pushed him off her very gently and turned over, raising her ass toward him. He grabbed her hips, entered her from behind and seemed to go even deeper. Kim yelled out in delight as she grinded her hips back into him. He pushed harder into her and harder. The deeper he seemed to go, he felt his dick swell to its peak, like it would explode at any moment. He could feel the cum rising.

He pulled out and turned Kim over, facing him. "I want to look into your eyes."

Kim kissed him, pulled him into her and screamed softly in his ear. "I'm cumming."

Lui raised his forearms, looking into her eyes. His dick released all he had built up, and Kim's eyes fluttered in her head as he did. She fell back, panting, and Lui looked at her, kissed her, then laid on her chest. She responded by wrapping her legs around his waist and continued to grind, cumming again.

When she released, she rubbed his back. "Lui…I…"

"Shhhh, say nothing…rest, just rest," he said.

Kim smiled, then laid back and not long after, fell asleep in his arms for the first time in days, peacefully.

DEAN HAMID

CHAPTER FOURTEEN

"That damn Sen Hong!" Tran spat as he rammed his fist down on his desk. "When will he just learn to mind his own damn business!" He pressed the intercom. "May-May, get me Trang on the phone!"

Trang was outside drilling his men when he got the call. He rushed into his office. "Yes, Dai Low!"

"Trang, Sen Hong has the girl."

"So, I've heard."

Tran got up from his desk and looked out the window overlooking the newly gentrified Cass Corridor area and said, "We need to get the girl."

"But, how?"

"The woman, uh, Kim, right?"

"The one who's been hiding the child."

"Yes, we need to get at her. She'll let us know where the child is if she's not with her."

"But, isn't she there with Sen as well?"

"Hmmm..." Tran thought of ways to get to them.

He thought back to every time he'd gotten close, and how every time it seemed he'd notified Trang, she somehow got away. He pondered on that for a second, then frowned face. "Let me think on it for a while, Trang...I'll get back with you."

"Okay, Dai Low, I'll be here."

Tran hung up the phone and called May-May again. "I need to step out for a minute. Have the car pulled around front."

Trang put down the phone, then sat thinking to himself. What was Tran up to? He picked up the phone and dialed. "Sen, Tran is up to something, he didn't say. But be careful and secure the surroundings, he might try something."

"I will," Sen Hong answered. "Keep me posted."

"I will. When is Vinny Ta coming in?"

"Should be this week sometime, keep an eye on Tran's whereabouts."

"I will."

"Trang!"

"Yes."

"Remember, stick to the plan."

"Definitely."

****

Sabo was walking towards the parking area when he spotted his partner coming into the precinct. "Hey, Pete, grab a cup of joe. We need to make a run."

Pete checked his watch and said, "This early…where're we going?"

Sabo smiled and said, "Early bird gets the worm."

Pete grabbed his coffee mug and walked over to the coffee pot, mumbling something under his breath to the effect, "*Damn the early bird…*"

"What'd you say?" Sabo smirked as he looked over, trying to suppress his grin. "Said something?"

"No…nothing, just get the damn car, will ya?"

Sabo stepped outside and grabbed the keys from the pound sergeant. He found the car he was looking for and opened the door, waiting for Pete to come out. Pete finally stepped off the stairway coming from the office and made it over to the car.

He got in, took a swig of the coffee, and asked, "Okay, where to?"

Sabo handed him a paper, and Pete read off the address, "Seven-ninety-eight, Woodward Avenue."

"Yeah."

"Who lives there?"

He took the paper back and pointed to the name. "Fred

Williams."

"Who's that?"

"The girl that's hiding out the little Asian girl. That's her father's address. We're going to check him out, see what he knows."

Pete spilled some coffee on himself. "Damn!" He tried wiping it off his shirt, and Sabo said, "Damn, Pete, what's wrong…you alright?"

"Hey, give me a minute, I need to get some napkins quick. Wipe this down."

Sabo sighed and said, "Okay, go ahead, but be quick. I want to get at this guy. He might go to work early. Then I'd have to find out where he works and all that, and we might not be able to get at him until tomorrow. If we're lucky."

"Okay, give me a minute." Pete stepped out the door and rushed through the stairway opening leading upstairs to the office.

He dipped into the bathroom and snatched up some napkins, then peeked out the door. He snuck over to a phone and dialed some numbers. When the person picked up on the other side, he said, "Tran, I'm on my way to that chick's father's house now. Sabo's on to something. You need to snatch him up quick if that's what you're going to do. I'll try to delay him, but it's going to be tight."

"Okay…I'm on my way out the door now."

Sabo pulled up in front of the walk up where Kim's father stayed, a small, two-family house. Since his wife left him, he stayed there doing what he'd been doing for the last thirty years or so. He went to work when he could, then came home and took a shower. He'd walk outside some, mostly just around the neighborhood, then just the house when the neighborhood got too dangerous. He spoke to his neighbors, at least the ones who were still there.

Many had left Detroit for places that had employment, where they could stay employed and have a pension at the end.

He continued working construction for the same company, but he was older, so much of his work was delegated towards cleanup, which he wouldn't have minded if his pay hadn't decreased as well. Younger men were now taking his place.

But still, he continued to strive. Every now and then, Kim would visit him, and they'd talk. Mostly about old times with her mother. She'd stay until his rantings began. But not before she bought food, checked his hygiene, and surveyed the house for small things such as bad plumbing, bugs, heating and air and all that. He also had her pay whatever bills that were needed, mostly his insurance mainly.

Rent was taken care of by the older woman downstairs, his landlord. She'd been there for years, Ms. Mary. She'd come up and talk to him while cooking him a good meal and play a little checkers, which she loved until he started to rant. For the most part, he was okay. At times, his mind would drift. Possibly early onset dementia, but otherwise he was okay.

When Sabo and Pete got out, they noticed the door into the house was wide open on an otherwise chilly day in a crime-ridden neighborhood.

They looked around outside and eased towards the door, calling out, "Is anyone here?" No answer.

Sabo unbuttoned his jacket and flipped his holster open. Pete did the same and they eased in, and another door was wide open, Ms. Mary's.

This time, they drew their weapons and called out, "Hello." Sabo pulled out the paper, looking over it for a name. "Ms. Mary…hello, is anybody home?" Still, no answer.

They walked inside the house cautiously and saw nothing amiss in the front room, the bedroom, and finally the kitchen. Then, they heard a noise coming from the laundry room. Pete led in first with Sabo right behind him. They heard it again and gradually opened the door and pointed their guns toward it. Two cats were trapped on the back porch. Pete opened the door and looked around the yard. He literally almost tripped over her. She was sprawled out on the back steps. Ms. Mary had been bludgeoned. Sabo reached down to check her pulse. Her body was still warm, and blood still ran freely.

Thinking whoever killed her might still be in the house, Sabo peeked over at Pete and motioned upstairs. He eased inside the house with Pete checking the outside. When he came through the door, Sabo was already up the stairs. The door had been kicked in. He eased in with Pete right behind him. They cased the house and found no one.

Pete called out to Sabo from the kitchen and pointed to the stove. "Look like he was making a quick bite, stove's still warm."

Sabo spotted a bag on the kitchen table. "Probably making himself lunch."

"Yeah, wouldn't doubt it," Pete said as he looked inside the bag."

Sabo put away his gun and said, "Somebody snatched him up. Either it's a damn coincidence or someone knew we were coming, hell, they just left."

Pete peeked out the back window through the shades and spotted a latch door at the end of the backyard that led to the alley. More than likely, Tran or his people took him to a car waiting out back.

He nodded. "Yeah, but who?" He made a mental note to close the latch when they went back down.

Sabo walked out to the car and picked up the radio to call it in. As Pete got in the car, he said, "Pete, we've got a mole in the department. I thought it might have been a coincidence, but now I'm thinking a whole hell of a lot differently. Someone's tipping these people off."

"But who?" Pete asked innocently.

"Don't know, Pete, don't know. But we need to find this guy. I'm thinking they snatched him up to get at the girl. And, once they get the girl…" He peeked back at the house, particularly Ms. Mary's place, and said, "They'll kill them both."

Before the squad cars and the boys from homicide would arrive, Pete and Sabo scoured the area looking for any clues. Sabo walked a little way up the block, and Pete walked the perimeter of the house. He came upon the latch door attached to the fence he'd seen earlier and stepped into the alley.

He spotted a black Maybach parked about fifty feet or so. He recognized it, so he squinted a little, staring into the windshield trying to get a peek inside, and the inside light came on. It was Tran. He nodded at him, then the car cranked up, did a U-turn, and drove off.

Pete stepped back through the yard, and Sabo walked up behind him. "Who was that?"

"Uh, nobody. Came out a backyard up a way…old folks. Didn't see anything suspicious."

Sabo was about to say something else, but the way Pete breezed by him, he was hesitant. Something was strange about it, he was a little off. "C'mon, Sabo, looks like a few cars are coming. We'll need to be out front when they arrive."

Sabo nodded. "Okay." He looked over at the fence. "I'll be right there."

"Yeah, hurry up!" Pete called out as he stepped around front.

Sabo unlocked the fence and stepped into the alley. He looked down in the direction Pete was telling him and didn't see any garages. At least any that were attached to homes that weren't either dilapidated or abandoned. He shook his head, thinking, why would Pete say that? He turned and started to step back through when he looked down. A trench, like something or someone, had been dragged. He followed the tracks, and they came from the back of the house. Someone had been dragged out of the door. It had to have been the old man.

He kneeled closer there were two sets of footprints. One small and the other large. A heavy man and a small man perhaps. They led into the alley. The dirt from the bottom of

Cold Hard Wind

the shoes stopped and disappeared. Like someone got into a car. He looked up, and Pete called his name, telling him to hurry. He walked through the gate and locked it behind him.

As he passed the covered body of the woman, he thought to himself, *'She must have put up a fight. Looks like she was running out back...maybe behind them.'*

He continued walking past her, vowing he'd avenge her murder. As he came into the front, he ran into Mike, his buddy from homicide.

"What's up, Sabo...gang related?" he asked.

Sabo looked toward the backyard and said, "To tell you the truth, Mike... I don't know...yet." He walked past him a little, then turned back, saying, "Hey, give me a call when you finish."

"Will do, buddy," Mike said as he slipped on his latex gloves. "Will do."

Sabo walked to the car, still pondering on what he'd seen. Pete was already inside. "So, what's up, what took you so long? The scene belongs to homicide now, I already briefed them."

"Yeah, that's good...nothing, just talking to Mike."

"About what?" Pete asked inquisitively. He also knew something was off with Sabo as well.

He glanced over at Pete and answered, "Whether or not it's a gang situation, or a homicide, kidnapping. That sort of thing."

"Can't really say yet."

Sabo glanced over again at Mike, then the house, and cranked up the car. "Well, I don't know...I think I can...I think I can."

"We'll see."

"Hey, look, I'm going to drop you off at the precinct. I'll catch up to you later."

"Sure, I can start the report. But Sabo, what's on your mind?"

"Aw, nothing really." Sabo lied he indeed had something on his mind, *his mole*.

Tran pointed his driver up 12 and 13 Mile, looking for

various shortcuts to maneuver away from where they were. His driver knew Detroit as well, if not much more than Tran, who was getting on his nerves, but he was trying to be patient with him.

They had arrived at Kim's father's not too much longer before Sabo and Pete. He picked up Lam, he needed someone fast. He was the man for the job. He owed Tran and needed to redeem himself from earlier. He really didn't have a choice. Afterward, they watched as Pete and Sabo arrived and went into the house. They dared not move, not wanting to bring any unwanted attention toward themselves. Once Pete stepped out and gave him the nod, it was only then did they leave.

Fred struggled and for that, he was punched a few times in the head. Otherwise, he remained quiet. They arrived at their destination. An old abandoned warehouse on the West side of Detroit. One of his commercial properties on John R Street.

His driver and Lam got Fred out of the car and followed closely behind Tran. He pointed them towards a doorway, and they walked through, entering the furthest back room. Tran pointed them toward the back and ordered them to tie the man up.

He took out his cell phone and dialed Trang. "Okay, I've got the old man. Send a message to Sen Hong. Release the girl...or I'll kill the man."

"I will."

He turned toward his driver. "Sathit, park the car around back out of sight. We might get some company." He looked over at Lam and ordered, "Call your boys." He tossed him the phone. "Tell them where to come, have them park around back... now. Oh, and another thing..." He stepped up to his face, staring into his scared eyes. "...if you get this right, I'll give you and your boys exclusive control over the Asian population here...and outside of Michigan. My word!"

After Lam ducked near a window getting some privacy, Tran walked over to the old man and just stared.

Fred heard his footsteps and shouted, "I know who this is!"

Tran backed up, frowning. "Who then?"

"My wife sent you after me…I know it!"

Tran looked at him oddly and laughed. "Yes…your wife." He walked away.

"You won't be laughing later. You or her, I know this was her doing!" he yelled, as his empty threats echoing throughout the old dusty empty building.

The only ones in fear were the pigeons that took flight as a result.

DEAN HAMID

CHAPTER FIFTEEN

Sen Hong received the call from Trang telling him what Tran had said. His reply was to be as expected. *'Tell him to kiss my ass!'* He then explained to Trang that this was a perfect time to take him out.

"Should we put the police onto him?"

"Not yet, I want to kill him myself. Then, we'll call them afterward and make it seem like it was a gangland assassination."

"But, what about the old man?"

"Bring him to me, his daughter is here." He thought for a second. "I might have the perfect plan for him."

"What?"

"Don't know for sure, but I might be able to use him to take out, Vinny Ta."

"Hmmm, I see…"

"Okay, Trang, I'll meet you at your place. I have to load up my men."

"I'll get mine as well…"

"No, Trang, if he sees them, that might set off an alarm. We'll use my people."

"I'll see you soon."

"Soon." He hung up and stepped out of his office into the restaurant, looking for Lui. When he found him, he told him, "Tran has kidnapped the girl's father."

"Damn! What do we do, Uncle!"

"I'm going to get him. I might have to pay a ransom. They really want the girl."

"Should I tell Kim…"

"Tell me what?" Kim had just walked into the restaurant area hearing somewhat of their conversation. Lui glanced over at Sen. "Something has happened to your father."

"What…is he all right?"

"Hopefully."

She moved closer to Sen, asking, "What happened?"

Sen sighed, he really didn't want her to know anything yet, but it was too late. "Tran has kidnapped him. He says your father, for the little girl."

"Oh no…"

"I'm not going for it, I'm rounding up some men now."

"Okay." Kim started to step away. "Let me get my jacket."

"No!" Sen yelled. "It will be too dangerous…you stay!"

"But, that's my father."

Lui stepped toward her and said, "Watch Alika, keep her protected. I'm sure Sen has everything covered, trust him."

She looked over his shoulder at Sen and said, "Okay, just take care of it, and please, don't let my father get hurt. He's all I got."

Sen nodded, then turned to go back into his office. "I won't, at least, not yet."

****

Sabo dropped Pete off and pulled back out of the lot, heading toward Old Chinatown. He had a hunch he wanted to check out. Turning the corner on Piquette Avenue, he slowed down and parked right up the street from Trang's spot. The old firehouse. He laid low in the vehicle, checking out the activity. People buzzed around the place, moving in and out. Cars pulled up out front, all four-door sedans and old-school Buicks, easy to ditch.

They backed into the apparatus bay of the fire station. From what Sabo could see, the trunks of the cars were opened. Then with some movement about, the trunks were closed. Four men got in, and they pulled out in front. Approximately four times, and four different cars. Twelve different men got into the cars. Tran's car pulled up front, and Trang and two other men got in, most likely his personal bodyguards. His car pulled out front, and the other cars lined up behind him, and they all took off.

Sabo knew from his personal experiences dealing with the Asian gangs, that many men meant something was going down. He also knew the activity involving the trunk could also mean they were loading weapons. That much he deduced. He watched as the cars pulled out and drove past. He lowered his head when they did, then glanced through the rearview mirror, watching the direction they went.

He cranked the car up, let them get about a block or so away then made a U-turn and followed behind. He felt down on his ankle for his backup and reached into the glove compartment for a handheld radio. He definitely needed to keep that on hand in case he needed to call for back up. Right now, he didn't feel it was necessary. His hunch told him there was more to what was going down.

He followed closely behind, but not so close as to attract any undue attention to himself. They took I-75 to the Northside and went up Woodward Avenue. They pulled over abruptly and parked. They seem to wait for some time, then they all eased out at the same time and went to their trunks and opened them. Sabo was right, they took out automatic weapons. Whatever it was, it was going down.

Sabo looked further up the street from them and spotted the building they were possibly going to. Out front were at least three men who stood guard. He didn't see any cars up front, but that didn't rule out the fact they may have been parked around the back. Trang's men dipped off the sidewalk into an empty, grass-strewn lot going towards the back of the warehouse. Sabo reached for the radio.

He hesitated, then thought, '*If Kim's father's in there like my hunch is telling me, I damn sure don't want to agitate the situation more than it already looked like it gonna be.*'

He had to find a way in and not get him killed. He pulled

out his .40 Cal, loaded the clip, and stuffed another clip in his jacket pocket. He took a few deep breaths and opened the door. Staying close to the backside of the sidewalk, he hunched down, creeping cautiously up the street. The neighborhood consisted mainly of old factories, like metal shops. Places where they manufactured car parts. There was no activity on the streets, albeit a few trucks that went by, making their way to the highway, but nothing to set off any bells. He crept up slowly behind their vehicles and looked in. They were all gone, he ducked off behind a trash dump and peeked out.

Tran's cars were all parked there, and a few of his men looked to be on patrol around the back area, behind a few abandoned trailers. They hand signaled each other. From what Sabo could deduce, they were letting each know who they needed to take out. Sabo ducked down, scanning the building, looking for another way in. He couldn't make a move then, so he waited, almost patiently it seemed, for all hell to break loose.

****

Kim paced the floor upstairs while Alika watched cartoons on TV. This time minus the Ramen noodles. The cooks downstairs liked her presence, and all she had to do was go to the kitchen. They fed her abundantly, as well as played and laughed with her. It was all good, but right now, Kim was distraught. Her anxieties kicked into overdrive and were all over the place. She couldn't stay still since hearing about her father. She couldn't handle it, she wasn't in control.

She glanced over at Alika and told her she would be back. Alika nodded her head, paying her no real mind, her eyes glued to the anime she was watching on TV. Kim had learned one thing for sure about the building…it was actually safe. Most, if not all the tenants there were family, and the majority of them worked in the restaurant. So, she didn't have any issue with leaving Alika for a moment since she was only going downstairs to Sen's office.

She was just about to knock when she heard him talking rather loud on the other side of the door. She thought he was possibly on the phone, so she stepped back, figured she'd give him a minute or two. Then overhearing him rant made her nosy, and she put her ear up against the door. What she heard next also made her knees buckle.

"Of course, he has men there, Trang. Take them out..." Pause. *"...fuck him, kill him if you need to. Make it seem like it was a gangland hit..."* Pause. *"Get the old man out alive, I'm going to need him..."* Pause.

Kim grinned, he was talking about rescuing her father. She exhaled and was about to knock when...

"I can use him...frame him for killing, Vinny Ta when he gets here! Then, kill him, too. Make it look like, Vinny Ta was trying to kidnap his daughter or something..." Pause. *"...once I get the codes from the little girl. Hell, we can kill her, too! We won't need her anymore..."* Pause. *"...just do it, Trang, and then we'll have control here, and the borders going into Canada!"*

Kim backed away from the door, horrified. She rushed back upstairs. Her body trembled from fright, and her anxieties had kicked into high gear. What to do, her mind throbbed? She stopped and leaned back against a rail, taking deep breaths trying to control herself like she'd learned when she was a child. In and out, in and out. She had to get Alika out of there, now. Getting a little more control of herself, she started back up the stairs, opened the door, and ran straight into Lui.

"Lui! I'm so glad to see you!" She pulled at his arm and ran into the apartment.

"What's going on, Kim?"

She pulled clothes out of the drawers, saying, "It's real bad, they're going to kill us, Lui!"

*"Kill us...*what are you talking about?"

She rushed into the living room. "Alika, we have to go! Pull some clothes out!"

Alika hesitated, looking at her oddly. Kim peeked her head back out and yelled, "Now Alika, now!"

Lui had had enough. He walked into the room, grabbing a duffel bag and stuffing it with clothes. Glancing over at him, Kim said, "I thought he was a good guy!"

"Who Kim?"

"I thought he had our back!"

Lui grabbed her by the arm and stopped her. "Kim, who are you talking about, what's going on?"

She stopped, took some deep breaths to calm herself, and looked at him. "Sen, he wants to kill me and Alika. He wants to kill Vinny Ta and take over."

"What? That's crazy! Why are you saying this?"

"Lui, I heard it with my own ears." Alika came into the room with a bag and her jacket. Kim helped her put it on. "Look, I only know what I heard…we're out of here!"

Lui stepped in front of them and said, "No, hold up. Let me talk to Uncle Sen and see exactly what's going on. Please, just wait here until I get back."

Kim sat on the bed with Alika as Lui walked out the door. "Sweetheart, I would never do anything to harm you. I swear, but this place is not good for us. We have to leave now. Do you trust me?"

Alika looked deeply in Kim's eyes for what seemed like a good minute and then nodded. Kim smiled, they got up and eased toward the door and peeked out. Suddenly, Alika snatched away from her and ran into the kitchen, opening the cupboard. When she returned, Kim looked down in her hand…a couple of packs of Ramen noodle soups. Kim shook her head and laughed.

"Well, …it was good while it lasted."

Grabbing her hand, they eased toward the stairs. She looked down, and the only opening she knew leading out was going past Sen's office. She definitely didn't want to go that way. Looking up, she saw the sign marked *'Roof'* and *'Exit.'* If they got to the roof, they could go down the fire escape out back. She did remember seeing one. She looked down at Alika and grabbed hold of her hand.

"Let's go upstairs." They started up the steps toward the roof and opened the door.

After opening the door and easing out, making sure that they weren't seen, they headed over towards the fire escape and looked over the ledge. "Well, it seems solid." Kim eased back from dizziness. "I'm glad you're not afraid of heights…but, I am." She hesitated and took deep breaths again.

Alika peered over the ledge and looked back at Kim. She walked over to her and pulled at her hand gently, then eased her gradually over towards the fire escape, holding onto her arm. She gestured for Kim to follow her down the metal stairs.

Kim looked down, then at Alika. She could see it on her face, *'Do you trust me?'* Kim made her choice.

She followed closely behind her, holding her hand all the way down.

Lui hauled ass down the stairs toward Sen's office. He was livid. How dare Kim accuse his uncle of something as devious as that! No way, she was probably mistaken…she had to be. But once he found out what was going on from his uncle, he'd set Kim straight. Even though he was catching feelings for her, it worried him to see her get upset and frazzled so quickly. He definitely would have to help her control her anxieties if they were to be together.

He finally made it to Sen's office, and it was locked. He rushed to the kitchen and asked the manager if he'd seen him. The manager told him Sen left out the back. Didn't say where he was going, or when he'd be back. That worried Liu some, more from what he'd have to say to Kim now to keep her from leaving than anything. He turned and started toward the stairs, then he caught something off the corner of his eye that made him glance back behind him. Someone was coming out from the basement. He didn't recognize him, but he gestured towards the kitchen manager and held up a cigarette. Lui guessed he was telling him he was going outside to smoke. Nothing strange about that, he thought, but he did wonder if Vong was still down there.

It had been at least a day since they'd arrived, no way could his uncle have left him down there. He casually made his way over to the door and was about to open it when the kitchen manager turned his way and stopped him. He had to think fast.

"Uh…" He pointed toward the back door. "I'm just going to watch over him until he gets back." It would only work if Vong was actually down there.

The kitchen manager glanced over at the door, then him, and nodded for him to go ahead. Lui knew he wouldn't have even disputed him anyway because he was Sen's nephew, but he had to tell him something to cover his ass. Lui opened the door and eased slowly down the steps. A light was on, but it was dim in comparison to the darkened basement. The air smelled of cigarette smoke, and he figured the guy went outside to get some fresh air because the air down there was thick and heavy.

He glanced to the right and saw the backs of two chairs, one was empty. Sitting in the other was a dark-haired man wearing a headset. Nodding his head in musical rhythm, listening to some music from the cell phone in his hand. He didn't hear Lui as he came down the stairs. A little way off from him, Lui saw Vong sitting with his hands tied in front of him and a gag stuffed in his mouth. Some plates sat next to him on a small card table where they had fed him and a bucket by his feet where they let him relieve himself.

He eased cautiously behind the man, and Vong lifted his head and saw him coming. His eyes widened in surprise, then Lui put his finger up to his lips, telling him to be quiet. He did, but Lui messed around and kicked a can on the floor. It clanked and rolled in front of the other man sitting. He saw it and started to turn, but Vong shook, making himself a distraction for Lui. He turned and looked over at Vong.

He stepped to him and yelled, "Be quiet!"

Lui ducked down so not to be seen, but he was so into quieting Vong that he had enough time to rush up behind him and put him in a choke hold, cutting off his airway long enough to put him to sleep. He let him slump to the ground and rushed over to Yong, pulling the gag from his mouth.

Vong coughed, then said, "Lui, help me! Please, don't let your uncle kill me!"

It was the same rhetoric Kim was saying. He kneeled in front of him and said, "My uncle would never kill anyone."

"That's not so."

Lui stood and raised his hand to strike him, and Vong spat, "He wants to kill Kim...and the little girl, believe me."

Lui stopped, no way could both stories be a coincidence. He said, "Okay, start talking."

Vong looked up the stairs. "We don't have time. The other guy will be back, soon."

Lui looked up, then back at Vong. "If you try to run, I'll find you myself! And it won't be on friendly terms!"

"I promise."

Lui untied Vong, and he stood, stretching out his stiffened limbs. They dragged the unconscious man toward the back of the basement and tied him up. Afterward, the door upstairs opened. It was the other man. He came down the stairs and looked. When he didn't see Vong or the other guy he left down there to watch over him, he started back up the stairs. Lui tripped him up, and he tumbled back the stairs to the ground.

He hit the ground hard and started to get up, but Vong punched him in the head. Shaking it off, he sprang to his feet and rushed Vong. Lui caught him from behind and put him in the same choke hold as the other. He struggled furiously, but it was to no avail. He was knocked out like his buddy. They pulled him to the back and tied him up also.

Lui looked over at Vong and said, "Now, tell me what's going on."

Vong told him everything Sen had said.

****

Trang and his men were in place, ready for him to tell them when to go. Trang reached into his pocket and pulled out his cell phone.

He called Sen. "Okay, we're in place. You want us to go?"

"No, not yet, I'm on the way!"

"Okay, I'll wait until you get here."

"I'm right off Fisher Highway, I'll be there soon."

Trang signaled for his men to lay low. Trang eased up a little to get a better view, and that's when he felt it on the back of his head. Cold steel, pushing his head toward the ground, and all he heard next were the sounds of all his men bodies dropping. He turned his head toward them, and he saw men behind them shooting guns with silencers.

They seemed to come out of nowhere, but no, they were hiding off to the right when Trang and his men came through the lot. Hidden in the tall grass. When Trang and his men went past, they got up and followed closely behind them. It was a trap.

Sabo watched in horror as it went down in front of him. He eased back and felt a steel barrel on the back of his head as well. He just closed his eyes, considering that all of Trang's men were slaughtered. He just knew he was next, he felt a pain on the back of his neck, and his mind went blank.

Sen got off the highway and turned on Piquette Avenue coming up toward the side of the warehouse. He saw the cars, and they were empty. '*Good*,' he thought. He glanced over toward the front, and no one was outside now. He parked across the street, sat and soon after, his phone vibrated.

He answered it, it was Tran. "Ah, Sen, glad you made it."

"What…what are you talking about?"

"Sen, do you think I got where I am by being a fool? And

someone else's fool at that." He laughed. "Look up at the roof." Sen peeked out the window of the car and looked up. Trang was pushed towards the ledge by someone that had a gun to his head.

Tran said, "Yes, he thought I was a fool as well."

"Look, Tran, I don't know what you're talking about."

"Then, why are you here…maybe, to watch this, huh?"

Trang was shot point blank in the head, and his body was pushed over the side and landed on the concrete below. Sen turned away at the sound of the sickening thud when he hit.

Tran said, "I'm going to let you live, even though I should kill you, right now. But go, secure the girl. Let me know when Vinny Ta arrives. We can continue with the same plan you had with Trang." He laughed. "Now, go! Oh yeah, by the way, can you clean up the mess downstairs for me? At least take the body, my men will clean up the rest."

Sen shook his head perplexed. *How the hell did he know? And, now what would he do without, Trang? He didn't have that many men. And, if Tran did know the whole plan behind taking out, Vinny Ta…would he tell him?*

****

Lui's teeth grinded hearing what Vong had told him. He couldn't believe it, but it must have been true. There were too many facts and details. His next thought was why? Why would he do such a thing? But it was too late for that now, he rationed.

Turning towards Vong, he asked. "What do we do now?"

"I really don't know, Lui, this is big." Lui walked away from him towards the stairs.

Vong stopped him and asked, "Where are you going?"

"I might as well let Kim know she was right."

"No, well, I don't mean it like that. I mean, we or I just can't go up the stairs like that. Those guys up there know what's going on down here. And, me being free would set off bells."

Lui stopped. "You're right."

"And, if your uncle comes back…no telling."

"We need to make a plan." Lui walked closer towards him and looked him straight in his eyes. "But I need to know you're with me this time…one hundred percent."

Vong paused. "Okay, I am, I want to get back at these guys anyway." He turned facing Lui and then said, "Especially your uncle…sorry nothing personal."

Lui just smiled. "Trust me…I know the feeling, none took."

"You have to go upstairs first. I'll stay down and keep an eye on these guys. Get Kim, and we'll go from there. Leave this place." Lui turned to go upstairs. "Oh, yeah, we're going to need a car." Lui gave him a thumbs up and walked up the stairs.

Vong knew that whatever they were going to do, it would be dangerous. But he also figured as long as they had Alika, they wouldn't be harmed, being that they needed her. At least, he hoped. Somehow or another, he also needed to get in touch with Vinny Ta.

CHAPTER SIXTEEN

He opened the door and turned toward the kitchen, looking for the manager, giving him thumbs up. As he opened the door going towards the stairway, he ran straight into Sen Hong.

"Going someplace?" He poked something into Lui's back that felt like a gun, then pushed him back toward the kitchen area. He looked down into the basement and called out, "Vong, you might as well come up, too!"

At first, Vong hesitated, then Sen yelled, "*Now!*"

He peeked his head up the stairs and slowly walked up the steps. Sen nudged him toward Lui, then gestured toward the kitchen manager who nodded back at him. Lui could only assume he was the one who'd told Sen he was down there in the first place, and the rest Sen just put together.

He pointed them towards his office and Lui said, "Uncle, why are you doing this?"

Sen smirked and said, "It's bigger than you, Lui. Actually, I was hoping you'd join me."

"In what, murder!" Vong spat.

Sen smacked him upside the head. "Shut up, I should have taken you out before."

He reached into his pocket, keeping an eye on them, and took out his key. He opened his office and ordered them inside. Looking behind him, he closed the door and directed them to some chairs next to his desk.

He sat and said, "Okay, so, now you know what's going on?"

Lui sighed and said, "Why kill the girl? You'd have everything from Tran. It would all be yours. *Why kill the girl?*"

Vong frowned and said, "Lui, he doesn't just want the money. He wants it all...everything, even Vinny Ta! Can't you see?"

Sen turned his way, saying, "You're smart, I will say that about you. But your smartness is also a threat." He turned back toward Lui. "Your friend is right, I want it all."

"But, why!"

"*Why!*" Angrily, he leaned forward and slammed his fist down on the desk. "Vinny Ta is not the man you think he is." He leaned into him. "That bastard is literally a slave owner, and he owns us…as his slaves."

"But look at all he's done for us…*for you!*"

"*Done?*" Sen got up from the desk, walked around front and leaned back on it. "Done for us, huh?" He shook his head. "Let me tell you a little something about, Vinny Ta…your grandfather."

"What…*grandfather?*"

"Yeah, Vinny Ta is your grandfather. Your mother's father."

"What are you talking about? She never…"

"Of course, she never, he kicked her out into the street."

"Why?"

He smirked. "She was caught fooling around with that American, the soldier from the US Army. It wouldn't have been bad if she would have just dated him, but no, her stupid ass thought she was in love, and ended up fucking him!"

Lui hung his head. "You're lying…he loved her."

"Lying, look at you. You are the bastard child of a nigga!" He got up and stood in front of him. "Her father was an influential man. It caused the family shame and dishonor. He had no choice but to put her out of the house."

"Fuck you!" Vong shouted at him.

Sen turned his way and smacked him. "But she was still his daughter. Deep down, he still cared for her. So, he secretly arranged for her to leave the country and come to America…here to me."

"Why you, are you her brother?"

Cold Hard Wind

Sen laughed, he walked over to a photo album and opened it, then turned some pages, and plucked a picture. He walked back over to Lui and tossed it at him. Lui reached down and picked it up. It was a picture of his mother, his brother, and sister. There was a man next to them.

He stared, then looked back up at Sen. "You!"

"Yes…me," he said, gritting his teeth. "She was my wife, she cheated on me. To avoid me from killing her, Vinny Ta sent me here." He turned away from him. "Your mother was a whore…she shamed me."

"But…" Tears welled up in his eyes.

"I only sent for her because I'd heard of the struggles she was going through. The kids…my children…you. So, I made a deal with Vinny Ta to have you all sent here. Vinny Ta, in return, would give me control…*power*."

"Hold up," Vong said. "So, the little girl, I thought she was Vinny Ta's granddaughter."

Sen looked at him and laughed. "You see, your friend here is smart.

"Yes, Vong, she is."

"Then, that makes her mother…"

"My sister-in-law."

"Oh, shit."

"Yes, oh shit indeed. Her husband was supposed to help us launder money for the Hip Chong Tong. They had no idea we, her husband Vien, was skimming thousands upon thousands. Vien had told me about the code. Hell, I kept him safe…the family. But, that goddamn Tran, he got greedy and reckless. Let the Tong know about, Vien. So, they killed him…*the whole family*."

"Why didn't you say something!" Lui yelled out.

"Why, so they could kill me, too? So, I would lose all that Vinny Ta had given me…what I had earned?" he spat, clenching his fist. "No, just direct it all towards Tran. Let him eat it, it was a good plan. Trang would be my lower boss, and we would rule together. The money coming in from the East Coast and Canada alone would make us wealthy men in this part of the country and back home in Laos!" He walked back around his desk. "Trang slipped too, but I will avenge him."

"How…what?"

"Once Vinny Ta comes here to retrieve the little girl, I will get the other half of the code. Kill him, then Tran, and once I do that, I take over. Even take Vinny Ta's own plane back to Laos and proclaim myself, The Chuk Sut." His eyes bulged at the greed pulsating in them. He looked over at Lui. "I can make you rich as well. You can be the Dai Low over here. Control all the interest, you'd be rich." He turned towards Vong and asked, "That's what you want, right?"

Vong just shook his head. "Yeah, I did, still do." He turned towards Lui and said, "But not at this cost…murder…deception. No…not at this price!"

Sen jumped up from his chair. "You've made your bed then! We go upstairs and get the girl!"

Lui jumped up from his chair as well and yelled, "No!"

Sen picked up his gun and pointed it his way. "Then…you can die."

"No!" Vong said. "We'll go."

"Smart man." He pointed them to the door and said, "Let's go!"

They stepped outside the office with Sen closely behind, with his hand in his pocket holding onto the trigger of the .38 he carried. He stopped for a moment to peek out into the restaurant area. There were a few people dining and a couple of people at the bar, nothing that warranted his attention.

Every now and then, he would get a crowd. Mostly weddings and celebrations of some sort. He wanted to expand downtown into the new growth coming up in the populace, the gentrification was starting to take place. Along with that, there would be an opportunity for new business, and of course, with that came *'habits.'* Habits ranging from marijuana to heroin. The popular drugs of choice for the up and coming generation.

He'd be able to mule much of that heroin in from Vietnam: Laos and utilize his people coming in. Also, his supply would be brought directly from suppliers across the water in Canada, he had it all figured out.

They came out of the stairwell heading towards the apartment where Kim was staying, and as they got closer, they noticed the door was still open, half cracked. Lui peeked in and called out Kim's name. Nothing, he called out Alika's name as well and still nothing.

Sen looked around inside and said to Lui, "Where are they!"

"I really don't know, she was here when I left."

Sen stepped back out the door. "We'll check every apartment on this floor if we have to. She's got to be here."

Vong peeked inside and noticed the dresser drawers open and all the clothes were gone. As he walked around, he noticed some hygiene products also missing. He went to the cupboard and found no food.

He stepped out of the apartment and caught up to Lui and whispered to him, "She's not here."

"What?"

"She's not here." He grabbed his arm. "Trust me." He glanced over towards Sen. "What do we tell him?"

"Shit, I don't know."

"What did Kim tell you?"

"She told that…"

Sen walked up on them and pushed Lui aside. "Told you what?"

Lui sighed and answered, "She told me what you were planning. That she knew you wanted to get the little girl."

Sen backed up, cussing. "Damnit!" He rubbed at his chin then looked over at Vong. "Do you have any idea where she went?"

Vong raised his hands. "I really don't."

Sen looked at them and threatened, "If you're lying, I swear…"

Vong pleaded, "No, I really don't know!"

He pushed past them and said, "I'll be back, don't go anywhere." He rushed toward the stairway.

Vong leaned back against the wall and blew, "Your uncle is crazy."

"Uncle, my ass," Lui said. "I can't believe all this."

"Look…" Vong told him. "You can call your grandfather and warn him."

"Then what? Sen's crazy enough to kill me and my whole family if he finds out. And my grandfather would surely call him."

"True."

"We need to find out where Kim went with Alika."

"Somewhere safe, knowing Kim," Vong said. "Somewhere no one would think of looking." He walked off then stopped, punching his fist into his hand.

He turned towards Lui and said, "I think I know."

"Where?"

"Can we get out of here?"

"I'm sure we can, but like I said, Sen is crazy."

"Once we get the girl, we can make the call to, Vinny Ta."

"Okay." He opened the door to his apartment and walked toward the window, he pointed at the fire escape. "We can sneak out. I'm sure Sen has people watching the doors downstairs, so this is our best bet."

They climbed out the window down to the ground, then Lui said, "Now, where to?"

"North-end Detroit."

"North-end Detroit…why?"

"That's where Malana lived."

"Wonder why she'd go there?"

****

Cold Hard Wind

The cab pulled up in front of a gate going up the driveway to the small mansion where Malana and Vien lived. The cab driver looked back at them and asked, "Is this the place?"

"Yes," Kim answered and stepped out the door.

The cab driver opened up the trunk and said, "Well, I would help bring the bags in, but the gates look locked. Is there anyone inside?" He looked around, peeking up the driveway. "It's pretty dark out here. You sure you want me to leave you here by yourself?" He looked down at Alika. "Especially with the child."

Kim grabbed the bags and said, "Right here is good, we'll be alright." She paid him.

After scratching his head and looking around, he shrugged his shoulders, got back in the cab and sped off.

Kim and Alika turned toward the gate. Kim looked at both sides. "We're going to have to climb over. I definitely don't want to leave you out here."

Alika glanced around and shook her head in agreement. They walked toward the right side of the gate where a patch of Asian honeysuckle bushes on both sides was bedded.

They looked behind them. "Alika, you can probably squeeze through." She looked up top. The black iron was smooth, and a thin bar sealed the bars of iron going upward. "I'll have to climb over. But, where? There's nothing for me to boost up on. And the metal is too thin to try to climb up."

Alika pointed down from them at a tree. It was just about as tall as the fence and had branches hanging across. Kim looked and sighed. "Heights...always heights."

They walked over to it, and Alika pointed up at an overhanging branch that stretched across the top of the fence. Kim could climb it, but she needed a boost up. Alika walked over toward the tree, looked it up and down, then beckoned her over.

Kim snickered and said, "Really, what type of games did

you guys play? Climbing…heights…"

Alika clasped her small hands together, and Kim put her foot inside them. Alika pushed up as hard as she could. It was just enough. Kim grabbed hold of a limb and pulled herself up. Struggling, she finally made it toward the branch overhanging over the fence.

She looked down at Alika and said, "Okay, squeeze through, don't forget the bags." Alika squeezed through the fence and looked up at Kim. It was about a fifteen-foot drop to the ground. Alika motioned for her to hang from the end of the limb, then let go.

Kim answered, "Easier said than done, kiddo." She crept along the limb.

It got thinner the further she went out, but she finally cleared the top, going across the fence. She stopped, taking a deep breath, keeping her anxiety in check as she looked uneasy at the ground. She grasped onto the edge and swung herself off. She was just about to release when the limb broke. She screamed as she fell to the ground. She fell on her back and didn't move. Alika ran over, the grass hadn't been mowed for a long while and as Kim's luck would have, broke her fall. She got up, rubbing her butt, and Alika giggled.

Laughing, Kim glanced at her and said, "Oh…it's funny, huh?" They picked up the bags and walked up the driveway toward the dark house.

The house windows had white curtains up to them so that nothing could be seen from the outside. The big, double-oak doors had yellow tape crisscrossed along the front that marked it as a police crime scene. Kim didn't really want to break the tape but would if she needed to. Alika tugged at her hand instead. She pulled her around to the side of the house toward a doorway going inside a small indoor greenhouse. She turned the doorknob and found it open. They entered, Kim stopped and looked around, smelling the redolence of Bonsai trees and Lotus. The smell was reminiscent of Malana. She would smell like that all the time. Admitting that she spent a lot of time in this very place. It was a place of solitude for her, and as Kim and Alika stood, they could feel her spirit.

Kim pulled herself out of it, and Alika pointed her over towards another door. Opening it led to an area that had shelves with pots, bags of soil, tools, and gardening utensils. Alika pointed to another door, and Kim slowly opened it. It was the kitchen, inside, it was dark, but Alika stepped past her and made her way to a drawer where she pulled out a flashlight and brought it to Kim. Kim turned it on to get her bearings and looked down at Alika.

"Okay, you stay here. I'm going upstairs to your daddy's office. I'll be right back. You stay right here, okay?" Alika nodded her head.

Kim went up the stairs, and Alika stayed by the door, close, looking around, remembering the happier days with her family. It was just like any other evening. They had just finished supper. The servants had cooked up some hoisin sauce and duck. Her brother and sister had left the table, and she stayed behind, helping with the dishes. The nanny teased her playfully with the water and soap bubbles. Her father had gone upstairs to his office, while her mother hung around in the dining area. Some men had come through the door. Everything appeared to be safe. They asked about her father and then went upstairs. Her mother didn't think anything of it other than perhaps they were another of many strange men that had frequented the house.

She called for Alika, telling her it was time to take her bath. Alika followed her up the stairs into her room, where her brother and sister were already. Her mother ran the water. Malana's mood was somber as she kissed Alika and told her she loved her, all the while feeling the markings on her back, rubbing them. After that, it was sudden.

A lot of noise came from downstairs, she remembered screams and shots being fired. Malana told her to stay, and she ran out of the bathroom. Alika heard more shots, more screaming from her brother and her sister. Her mother came back in, picked her up and ran into the guest room. She pushed Alika inside the back side of the closet and told her not to move, no matter what. Alika saw two men she didn't recognize come through the door soon after with guns. They asked her mother questions, and she kept screaming, no.

Terrified, Alika dared not move, when they just shot her mother. They looked around, under the bed and even came toward the closet, looking around. Alika ducked down into the darkness, quiet, scared. They hadn't seen her and left. More shots, then it got quiet. Malana still had life in her, and she dragged her body toward the closet. Alika peeked her head out, and Malana told her to stay there. And, that's where she stayed until Kim came. It seemed like forever, but it had only been a matter of hours.

Alika stood there, taking it all in, not paying the tears running down her face any mind. Not even noticing her legs trembling so much until they buckled from under her, and she was in tears on the floor. Kim made her way up the stairs, going to Vien's office. She shined the flashlight around and noticed that the walls where the spots of blood were had been wiped clean, and the furniture covered. She opened the door to Vien's office and noticed the screen from the computer was lit.

"Good," she said. "The power's still on." She reached around the wall and flicked on a light switch, easing towards his desk. She searched through his Rolodex and his top drawer. She opened his files.

"Nothing," she said.

It dawned on her, okay, Alika's grandfather. She pulled out the kid's folder and opened Alika's. Her birth history, also, checking out her ancestry lineage, next of kin. There it was, Zhuge Long-xi, or *Vinny Ta.*' Alongside his name were numbers. Kim grabbed for a pen and paper and wrote them all down. Satisfied, she backed away from the desk and eased toward the light. She clicked it off and made her way downstairs.

DEAN HAMID

CHAPTER SEVENTEEN

Sen's car pulled up to the gateway a little after Kim had gone into the house. Lui, Vong, and his personal driver Chen got out. He still had the gun cuffed in his hand.

Lui pushed at the gate and said, "It's locked, there's no way in." He looked both directions, then up the driveway. "And, even if they were here. How would they have gotten in?"

Vong said to Sen, "You need a code." He glanced up at the security camera overhead. "I doubt it's working anyway. I don't even see a light on the camera. Why would it be on anyway? There's no one inside to protect."

Sen pointed them off to the side, and he looked up the driveway toward the house, at a big, black shadow. That's when he spotted it. "Look." He pointed. "Up there!"

A lone light shined in one of the windows. The light Kim had turned on in Vein's office.

"I don't know how they got in, and I don't care, but…" He reached in his pocket, pulled out a plastic card the size of a credit card and walked toward the intercom box set up at the gate. He swiped it through the opening on the side. The doors clicked for a moment, then the locks opened. He pointed them back to the car and had his driver push the gate open. He got back in and drove up the driveway.

Vong nudged Lui in the side and mouthed the words, "What the hell?"

Sen caught it and said, "Oh, yeah, that's how Trang got in that night."

Sen ordered his driver to stop a short way from the entrance, and they all got out and crept to the door under the cover of darkness. Sen had his driver keep cover on Lui and Vong. He approached the door, then looked in the side portals. It was dark, but he could still see the shine of the light from upstairs. He nodded, then told them to follow him. He went around the side through the same doors that Kim and Alika had gone through. He saw the door to the greenhouse leading to the kitchen had been opened.

He crept through and that's when he saw her. He reached into his pocket for his gun, but not before he heard the footsteps coming down the stairs and a light. He knew it was a flashlight. It had to be Kim. He snuck up behind Alika just about the same time Kim came into the kitchen. He grabbed her from behind and put the gun to her head.

He said to Vong as he came through the door and saw what was going on, "Your hunch was right."

Kim looked over at Vong and said, "Why did you tell him we would be here!"

Vong looked down to the floor, dejected. "I'm sorry...I didn't mean to..."

"Shut up!" Sen eased back to where his driver stood. "All of you, over to the side."

He pointed them into the living room and backed up slowly with Alika in his clutches. "Now, I'm going to take the girl." He glanced over at his driver. "But Chan here is going to make sure you all are no more problems to me." He snickered. "Actually, I'm glad I got you all here together. By the time someone notices you missing and finds your bodies, I'll be long gone." He laughed.

Kim lunged toward him, and Lui stopped her. "No, Kim, he'd just as easily kill, Alika."

"And peel the tattoo off her cold, dead body. Now, get back!"

"Uncle, why are you doing this?" Lui pleaded.

Sen tightened up on Alika's neck, trying to keep her from wriggling free, and said, "To get back at, Vinny Ta. To get back at all the people who wronged us!"

"They..." Lui pointed towards Kim and Vong, "...have nothing to do with this, at least let them go."

Vong added, "I won't tell anyone, I swear!"

Sen laughed. "Oh, you're definitely going to die. I might kill you myself. You're the king of lies! You'd tell on me if a dime was offered to you!"

"Fuck you!" Vong screamed at him.

Sen looked over at Kim and said, "If there is a regret, it's the girl. She's brave and noble, honorable." He shook his head then continued, "But her father is already a pawn."

"My father?" Kim hollered.

"Yes, Tran has him, and he's going to use him to kill, or at least frame him for killing, Vinny Ta. He's part of his plan, and I had nothing to do with that."

"Where is he!" Kim screamed out. "Please, tell me!"

"It's too late."

"He doesn't have anything to do with this, nothing! Why?"

"Because of you, that's why. Don't you see, when you got involved with this girl, this family, you were marked for death, and everyone you know." He glanced at Lui. "This just didn't start over here in this country. It's been ongoing for centuries."

"This is crazy, Vinny Ta took care of you, Uncle Sen!"

"Only because of your mother's involvement!" He glanced down at the girl. "Your cousin here was marked for death the minute she was born. Hell, it was supposed to be you!"

"Me?"

"Yes, you have his bloodline. Vinny Ta would have made you his successor, but your mother's behavior changed all that."

"But you have the little girl. Why can't you just write down the codes and let her go?"

"No, there's more to it. A language as well, but enough talk, I'm sorry…" Sen eased out the back door with the struggling little girl, and Chan moved out in front, raising his gun up at them.

Kim grabbed onto to Lui, and he hugged her.

Vong looked over at Kim and said, "I'm sorry…"

Sen backed Alika up through the door, she struggled with

him going through the door and as a result, kicked one of the large, metal shelves that held soil and tools. It tipped forward onto them. Sen put his hand up to catch it and let go of the girl. She ran. He called out to Chan for help, turning his attention away from Lui and the rest. That's when Vong lunged at him. He grabbed at the gun, and they both wrestled to the ground with it.

Vong managed to shout out to Kim and Lui, "Get out of here!"

"No, I'll help!" Lui said instead.

Vong kicked at Sen as he struggled and yelled out, "Get Alika and get out of here now, while you have the chance!"

Kim didn't hesitate, she grabbed at Alika and started for the door. Lui followed too, but then he doubled back and jumped on Chan as well, wrestling the gun out his hand. He got up off the floor and pointed at Chan after Vong pushed away from him. He fired, catching Chan in the chest, and he staggered backward.

Sen had finally managed to get the shelving off him and reached down for his gun, turning around.

Lui already had a bead on him and yelled out, "No, Uncle…don't!"

Sen wasn't trying to hear it. As he turned and pointed at Alika, Lui shot him. He pointed again as he fell backward, and Lui fired again. This time he was down, and the gun dropped out of his hand. Vong kicked it away from him. Lui ran over to him and kneeled over him. Blood seeped out of Sen's mouth; he didn't have much time.

Lui cried, "Why, Uncle? I looked up to you, you were my hero! *Why?*"

"I would have set you up, kid…put you on my team."

"No… no…"

"Where's my father!" Kim rushed over to him.

Lui said, "Please tell us…"

Sen looked up at Kim and said, "You would have made a

courageous Asian warrior." He grabbed at Lui's shirt and with his last dying breath, said, "I'll do it for you. The old Asian bakery over on Woodward Avenue. But, be careful…" His voice trailed off, and he died.

****

Sabo groaned as he awoke. Instinctively, he tried raising his arms, but his hands and legs were tied together on a metal office chair of sorts. A gag was stuffed in his mouth, and when he turned his head, he saw another man in the same predicament, also bound and gagged. He was out like a light. Sabo stared at him for a moment, trying to figure out his role in this matter. It dawned on him. He was the older black guy they were looking for, Kim's father. This was where he was taken. What he couldn't figure out was why? Maybe it was planned to have Kim come to him, with the little girl in tow? That sounded about right.

He stretched his neck around and grimaced from the pain on the back of his skull. He wondered who the hell knew he was coming. He heard some shuffling about in the next room and footsteps coming toward the door. He could barely see, but it was the silhouette of three men. The one in front stepped off to the side and flicked a light switch. The light poured into the cloudy, dusty, empty room, and he blinked a few times. Finally, he could recognize the figure: Tran.

Along with him was another Asian he recognized, who was short and scraggly with a ragged goatee. He knew him from his dealings with the gangs in Chinatown. He squinted his eyes, trying to see who the other guy was. He couldn't believe it: Pete.

Tran stepped toward him, saying, "Sabo…Sabo, you just had to push the envelope."

Sabo struggled to speak, but all that came out were muffled sounds. "Oh, how rude of me," Tran said as he leaned forward.

He reached out and pulled the gag from his mouth. "Well, there's no need for introductions here. I'm sure you know who everyone is." He turned toward Kim's father and said, "All except for him." He walked over to him and pulled his gag out as well.

Jumping out of his sleep, he looked around at the men standing in front of them and hollered, "I know she sent you to kill me…I won't talk! I won't tell you where our daughter is! I've got her somewhere safe!" Then he mumbled to himself.

Sabo looked up at Tran. "You no good, dirty son of a bitch!"

"Perhaps."

"You'll never get away with this."

"Really? Always the quips, you see…" He gestured for a chair and pulled it in front of him to sit, facing Sabo. "…get away with what, Sabo? You don't even have a clue as to what's going on…"

"Kidnapping a police officer for one!"

"Well, there's more to it than that. Yeah, but you'll never be kidnapped if there's nobody." He glanced up at Pete. "Or, if you were to have a deadly accident. We haven't quite figured that out yet."

"I can't believe you'd sell me out, Pete! After all, we have been through!"

Pete paced. "You're right, all we've been through. And, for what, Sabo…for what!" He reached in his pockets and pulled them inside out. "Empty pockets, we're chasing the bad guys, and they're getting away. You know why? Because guys like Tran here are greasing their pockets and making them rich. And, after all, we do, they still won't let a little of it trickle down." He backed up and turned away. "I'm tired of it already."

Tran smiled, listening to him rant. "He's smart, Sabo. Why should you guys do all the dirty work…for nothing?" He pointed toward Lam. "Look at Lam here. He was also an underlying…and yes…" He looked up at the burn marks around his eyes. "…I went a little too far, perhaps. But the point is, he's learned, he's grown. And he'll be running the Hip Chong Tong pretty soon. While your friend here would make an excellent chief of police."

"So, you'll just kill me."

"Well, I thought about it…and yes." He got up from his seat and walked out. "Yes, you'd never conform. Once a good cop, always a good cop."

Sabo turned toward Pete. "Pete, he's a snake, don't trust him!"

"I'm sorry, Sabo, I've made my bed." He turned and walked out as well.

Sabo hollered out, "One thing!" They stopped. "What about this guy?" He nodded toward Kim's father. "What role does he play?"

"Good question, Sabo," Tran said as he turned to face him. "He's the fall guy, he'll be the one charged with Vinny Ta's body."

"Why?"

"Because he's just the right amount of crazy." Tran laughed as he left out of the room.

The door closed and the lights switched off. He turned and looked at Fred. Fred stared back and said, "Don't worry, we'll get out of this."

Sabo lowered his head. "I sure hope so, buddy."

****

"So, what do we do now?" Vong asked.

Kim got up slowly from where she sat and rushed him, wrapping her hands around his neck, yelling. "*Why…why did you tell him!*"

Vong wrestled with her. "I didn't mean to!"

"You didn't mean to!"

Lui struggled to break them apart. "He didn't mean to!" He finally broke them apart and stood back to catch his breath. "We need to find a way to get in touch with, Vinny Ta. Let him know what's going on."

Kim reached into her pocket and pulled out the paper she had scribbled the numbers on. "I got some numbers." She showed them to Lui.

"Okay, phone numbers, let's call."

Kim reached for her cell phone and couldn't find it. She looked around for her bag. "Damn, must have left them..." She looked over at the entryway of the door going toward the greenhouse and pointed. "Over there." Rushing she stepped over Sen's body looking for the bags. She spotted them, but the one she was looking for was underneath Sen's body. She called Lui over, they pulled his body up off it and she searched around inside.

She found it and sighed. It had been broken when Sen fell on top of it. "Now what!"

"Okay, we still need to go to the warehouse. We have to get your father."

"That's right, I hope they haven't harmed him."

Vong hung his head down and paced the floor. "This is all my fault." Alika walked toward him, reaching for his hand. He looked down at her, and she smiled up at him. Vong said, "You've got a way with that smile."

Kim looked over and shook her head. "Vong, you just have to choose a side."

"I know, Kim, I did...the right side."

Lui nodded his head in agreement. "We still need a plan."

"We need to get to that warehouse, Lui. You know where it is, right?"

"Yeah."

"Okay. Let's move these bodies toward the greenhouse. Then call the police."

"Not yet."

"Don't move the bodies?" Kim asked.
"No, don't call the police…at least, not yet."
"Why?"
"We don't know how big this thing is." He looked at them. "Sen had a fucking security card to the gate, and he literally said Trang was the one who killed Malana and her family. C'mon now, you mean the police couldn't figure this thing out?"

"You got a point."

"We call them when everyone is safe. Kim's father and Alika."

"We still need to figure out how to get in touch with, Vinny Ta."

"We buy a throwaway once we leave her."

"Well then, let's go, C'mon, Alika. *Alika?*"

They looked around and didn't see her. Kim went upstairs to look in a few rooms. She found her in Malana's room, sitting on the floor crying as she stared at a picture of her family. Lui and Vong rushed upstairs and asked if she'd found her.

Kim nodded and said to them. "Yeah… but please, give her a moment. She deserves it…"

****

After piling up in Sen's car, they got on the road. Along the way, they spotted a couple of convenient stores open, but Vong kept saying he knew of one closer to where they were going. They drove I-75 and came up the rampway. After a few turns, they drove up behind the warehouse. The sun was just coming up.

They could see a few men out front. Even one that had a few bags of what appeared to be food going inside the building. Four cars were parked in front, and as they drove by, they saw a big splotch of blood on the concrete—Trang's. Lui pointed them up the street. He got out with Kim and Alika, and Vong told them he'd be right back. He was going to the store he spoke of earlier to buy a throwaway phone to contact Vinny Ta.

Vong drove off, and Kim, Lui, and Alika ducked into the lot close to the warehouse. The same lot that Trang and his men used to sneak up on Tran. But they were clueless of that. Unfortunately for Tran, he and his men weren't. Tran was notified and immediately he and Pete came down the stairs from the upstairs office to the back dock, watching as they crept forward. Tran ordered his men to back off and let them get close.

Tran heard a noise upstairs and motioned towards Lam to go upstairs to see what it was. More than likely, he thought the old man was probably ranting and might have rocked his chair over. He'd already done it before to break free. But Tran also knew from prior dealings that if you're going to tie a man up in a chair, it would be good for it to be a metal chair.

Lam crept his way upstairs toward the door, then slowly opened it. The old man was kicking and screaming in the chair on the floor. He had knocked it over. His head was tilted to the side and a white, milky substance spewed out of his mouth.

Sabo yelled out, "He needs help, he's having a seizure."

Lam looked behind him and stepped into the room. He didn't want to disturb Tran for something he felt was petty, and that he could handle himself. He didn't want to mess up his shot at being Dai Low of the Hip Chong Tong. He had to make decisions. He looked down at the old man wriggling about in his chair and thought, how serious could it be anyway. He got closer, and Fred's eyes fluttered up in his head, then he appeared to stop breathing.

Figuring he was dead and no threat, he loosened the restraints on him, and he slumped to the floor. Lam kneeled down over him and put his ear up against his chest for a heartbeat. That's when Fred sprang into action. He grabbed him and wrestled with him to the ground, yet at the same time, tried to keep his hand around his mouth so he wouldn't yell out. Lam was busy fighting him and trying to make a run for the door. Fred grabbed onto him with everything he had. Finally, he managed to put a choke hold on him, but Lam wrestled off him and tried to make another bead for the door.

Fred grabbed him and tripped him up, he fell on Sabo and knocked him over in his chair. They wrestled and fought, and at one point, Fred squared up with him and took a few licks and managed to hold his own. Once he got a grip on him this time, he wasn't trying to let him go. All the years of heavy construction made his arms and his grip tough as steel. He held onto him, but Lam busted free and Fred pushed him in the back as he tried to run, causing him to trip up. He scrambled and fell toward Sabo.

Lam grabbed hold of him again, but he couldn't steady himself as he got up and one more rush from Fred had him falling backward. His head hit the leg of the steel chair, and he fell out. He rushed over and saw that the back of his skull had been busted open by the now bloodied steel chair leg.

He looked at Sabo and shook his head. "Thought I was crazy, huh?" He untied Sabo and soon after, they were both free, peeking out the door towards the office and the stairs going down.

****

Vong purchased the phone and sped back to the warehouse. He drove through the front, cutting his eyes over in the front sidewalk. He also glanced inside the lot and watched as Kim, Lui, and Alika were being held and taken inside the loading entranceway. He allowed the car down a little, noticing that someone came out the front entrance, peeking at the car he was in. He sped up and, once he was a few blocks away, pulled over, trying to figure out what he should do.

He knew he had the phone, but with no numbers. He definitely wouldn't call the cops. That would be too dangerous for Kim. The warehouse was heavily guarded for him to just try to go inside without being caught or killed. But who? He banged on the dashboard in despair.

"So, you figured you'd pay us a visit," Tran smirked as Kim, Lui, and Alika was led at gunpoint into the building. He pointed them over to a loading bank and said to Pete, "Okay, keep an eye on them…I have to make the call."

"A call, to who?"

"It's all set in motion now. I have to pull, Vinny Ta into the picture now."

"Hope you're going to get in touch with him because Sen Hong never came back."

"Damn right!" Lui spat. "Sen Hong is dead!"

"*Dead?*" Tran stopped, then turned toward him. They walked slowly to him. "Why should I believe you?"

"How else would I have known to come here?"

Tran rubbed his head and turned away, pacing. "I'll just have to go in another direction then."

"C'mon, Tran, this was supposed to be foolproof!" Pete yelled out.

"Shut up, I need to think!"

Pete pointed to one of Tran's men to watch over the group while he went upstairs to the office. He pulled out a chair from the desk he'd been occupying and sat. He knew the only way to get out of this mess would be to call it in. But he'd have to kill Sabo, and definitely Tran. That was a lot. He'd have to gamble that no one would get out alive except for him. It didn't add up, but he needed to do something fast.

He decided he'd at least kill Sabo and the old man. He reached in the drawer for his gun and gasped when he didn't see it there.

He searched through the whole desk. Then, he heard, "Looking for this?"

Sabo had his gun pointed directly at him. "How the hell you let Tran convince you to take off your weapon? That's crazy!"

Cold Hard Wind

Pete kind of snickered and said, "I never put it back on when I came out of the room talking with you and the old man. That was my bad."

"Don't take your weapon into interrogation type of thing, huh? Once a cop, always a cop I guess, Pete. Too bad because you would have been one of the best ones too." He pointed him away from the desk. "Now get over there, and don't make no sudden moves." Sabo reached behind his back and pulled out his cuffs. "You left these, too, now, you know the drill!"

Pete put his hands behind his back and yelled out, "Where's my wife!" It wasn't much, but it distracted Sabo enough, so Pete had enough time to turn around to struggle with Sabo for the gun.

He knocked him to the floor, and the gun fell out of his hand. He tried to find it, but Sabo grabbed his leg, and he fell short of it. He then climbed on top of him and punched him in the face and head. Pete countered as best he could.

Sabo yelled over at Fred. "Get the gun!"

Fred ran over and picked it up. Just when he was about to aim, his legs buckled, and he collapsed. Pete and Sabo heard the shot but didn't know where it came from until Fred slowly slumped toward the floor. It was Tran. "How did they get loose!"

"Just get the gun and him off me!"

Tran looked down at him and eased toward the gun. "I can see you're going to be a problem." He kicked it across the room to the far corner then walked back toward the door. "Fend for yourself! I can always find another chief of police flunky! After all, they come a dime a dozen!" He slammed the door shut and ran off laughing.

Sabo and Pete faced off with each other, glancing over at the gun on the far side of the room. Sabo said, "Let it go, Pete, I'll see that you get a fair one."

"*A fair one*? I'll be crucified, and you know it! My pension, everything…gone! And, you know what, Sabo? I damn sure ain't going to no fuckin prison!" He lunged for it, and Sabo blocked him.

They crashed to the floor and wrestled. Pete was closer to the gun and reached for it, but Fred still had life in his body. He grabbed hold of him long enough for Sabo to reach the gun himself. Pete elbowed Fred in the face, and he fell off him. He looked at Sabo, but it was too late.

He climbed to his feet with the gun, pointed it at Pete, and said, "Don't make a move, Pete!"

He lunged, and Sabo pulled the trigger, Pete dropped. Sabo rushed over to him. "Why, Pete…why?"

"That's the way things go in this town…the way things go…" Those were his last words.

Sabo shook his head and rushed over to Fred. "You alright?" He felt around his back but didn't feel any blood until he felt his shoulder. "Good…the shoulder…"

"Yeah, winged me…"

"Okay, I'll get help, just hold on." Sabo got up and ran toward the door and Fred called out. "Get that fucka, he's got, my wife!"

Sabo shook his head and yelled back. "I will."

Tran's men heard the gunshots from upstairs and ran toward the stairway. "Go upstairs and kill them!"

Lui pointed Kim and Alika toward a back exit and told them to run, but it was too late. Tran was already on them.

"Give me the girl!" He pointed the gun at Alika. "Now!"

Kim was hesitant, but she let go of her hand, and Alika stepped forward. He grabbed her by the collar and started toward the front door.

He turned and told them. "I suggest you run. When my men come back down and sees you, they have orders to kill you on the spot!"

Suddenly, his cell phone buzzed. "Fuck…now?" He pulled it out and looked at the screen.

It was May-May. "Vinny Ta's private jet is at the airport."

"Vinny Ta…here?"

Lui looked over at Kim and whispered, "Vinny Ta is here already."

"My sister-in-law who works there told me. It's hush-hush, they have them in a private hanger."

"Okay, I'm on my way, call you when I get there." He hung up and stuffed the phone back in his pocket. "Maybe this might not be a bust after all." He turned toward the door and turned the knob. He opened it, peeked out and looked both ways, and he was gone.

Lui and Kim ran toward it as well. They watched as Tran ran with Alika in his clutches toward a car.

Lui looked back at Kim and said, "Let go after him! We know he must be going to the airport! We've got to warn Vinny Ta that he's walking into a trap!"

Kim glanced upstairs and said, "I have to get my father first."

"They have guns, we don't have anything!"

Vong stepped through the door. They looked at him somewhat startled by his sudden entrance. In his hand, he carried an aluminum bat. "I got the phone." He reached in his pocket and pulled it out. "I didn't know what to do. I came through and saw them snatch you guys up." He lowered his gaze, feeling somewhat shameful that he left them. "I didn't want to leave you guys, I had to do something." He picked up the bat. "This is all I could think of."

Kim just looked at him, listening, sympathetic to his feelings. She reached out and picked up his head and said, "That's okay, Vong, it's something."

"I couldn't leave you guys by yourself." He looked over at Lui. "Told you I changed, bruh."

"I believe you." Lui smiled.

Then, they heard footsteps coming down the stairway and turned toward the entranceway. They crouched down, ready to jump at whoever came through.

"Well, this is what it comes down to," Lui said.

Vong picked up his bat, ready to swing. Then, the footsteps came closer and when the faces appeared in front of them, they were thrown back in surprise.

Sabo led the way, with Tran's men behind him and Fred helping him along. Sabo saw them and said, "You guys are?"

Fred pushed forward and rushed for Kim. "My baby girl!" She reached out and grabbed him before he stumbled. "I'm her father."

"Dad, are you okay?" She rushed for him, gasping at the blood stain in his shirt.

"Hold up," Lui said baffled. "What the hell is going on here? Last thing I knew, Tran sent his men up to kill you guys, and now you're coming down like you're freaking buddies or something."

"Oh, uh." Sabo looked behind at the few men that Tran left behind and said, "Well, the deal was, when they came through the door and saw their boss dead, they were pissed. Don't get me wrong, I thought we were finished." He rubbed his head. "It got kind of touchy at first, but…" He pointed toward Fred. "Hell, Fred told them Tran had left them behind. Told them that I was a cop and if they killed us, they'd have to run for the rest of their lives. Tran didn't give a damn about them, and their boss was dead anyway."

"You serious?" Lui said as he glanced down at Fred.

"Yeah, they heard him out. I mean…he made sense!" He turned and looked at them. "This is what's left of the Hip Chong Tong in Detroit."

"Wow."

"I said the same thing, but it worked." One of them stepped up and said to Lui, "I'm Ting Ngo. Tran double-crossed us, and we're going after him."

Lui said, "I know where he went."

Sabo said, "Well, let's go, then."

Lui stopped him. "No, from here, it's Laotian business."

Ting nodded and said, "We can handle it."

"Nothing personal," Lui added.

"Okay, I understand, I have to call it in though," Sabo explained to them.

"That's okay, do what you do…just give us a little time."

"You guys get out of here." He turned toward Kim.

"You're going to take your father to the hospital, right?"

Kim looked up at Liu and hesitated to answer, then Sabo said, "I see…"

"Kim, you need to stay," Lui said.

"But, Lui, I owe it to Alika to see it out. Make sure she's safe…I owe it to Malana."

Vong helped to lift Fred and said, "Go, I got this, hurry, you guys."

Kim reached out, hugged Vong and kissed him tenderly on the cheek. "Thanks." She glanced back down at her dad and said, "I'll come to the hospital and…"

"Go…get your mother."

"Yeah, yeah, go, that's what friends are for. Now go!" Vong said.

Tran's men left with Lui and Kim, got in their cars, and sped off. Sabo stayed behind with Fred and Vong.

Vong said, "One hell of a woman."

"You should have seen her mother."

Fred said, "Mother…what I'd miss?"

Sabo answered Vong, looked down at Fred and said, "Trust me, long story…I'll be right back. I'm going to get my radio."

CHAPTER EIGHTEEN

Ting and his men came into the busy Detroit Metropolitan Airport by way of John Dingell Drive. They all jumped out and ran into the McNamara Terminal. Ting was the only one with enough sense to ask where Tran went.

Lui looked at Kim, and she shrugged. She was clueless as well. But she did mention that it would have to be somewhere kind of secluded. For a plane to come in unannounced. The look on Tran's face when he got the call that Vinny Ta was here indicated it definitely was unannounced. He was clueless.

Lui agreed, inside the terminal, he asked one of the baggage handlers, and they gave him a possible destination. The North Terminal D-32. Ting told them he'd catch up with his men and meet with Lui and Kim later. Kim pointed to a shuttle bus. They boarded, making their way to the north side of the busy airport hub.

Kim and Lui went the opposite way from Ting and his people. They found D-32 and the entrance going into the back of the hanger. Lui pulled at the door, finding it open. The offices inside the hallway going towards the hanger were dark, so it was easy for them to keep cover. Lui pointed toward the plane…a white Gulfstream G650 luxury jet. The lights were on inside the plane, and Lui figured he could make his way inside to talk to whoever was inside. He hesitated when he got to the plexiglass door leading out into the bay. He saw Tran, and in his clutches was on Alika. She seemed worn out and rightfully so. She probably struggled with him the whole way there. He eased up closer towards the ramp going into the plane and shouted something.

Lui opened the door slightly and heard some of what he said, "Vinny Ta…Vinny Ta!"

Cold Hard Wind

A big Asian man approached the door and asked him, "What is it you want?"

"I want to speak to, Vinny Ta!"

"About what, may I ask?"

"*May you ask*...may you ask!" He pulled the gun from his coat pocket and pointed it at Alika's head. "How about this, that's what?"

The big Asian disappeared back into the plane. One of the portal windows on the plane slid open for a minute. A moment later, a shadow appeared at the door. An old Asian man wore a grey suit tailored for his figure. He seemed to have the gait of a man in his forties, at least. He was cleanly shaven except for a long grey goatee that hung down to his chest. Kim had to ponder, was he really as old as they said he was? He couldn't be.

He stepped towards the top stair of the plane, and other men came out, stopping him. He waved them off with their disapproval and continued down the ramp. Tran watched him the whole way, keeping the gun to Alika's head as he backed away close to the underbelly of the aircraft.

Once Vinny Ta reached the bottom rung, he told him to stop. He did, then he said to Tran, "Why do you have a gun to my granddaughter's head?"

"I know about the codes. I know you have the end code, and I know about the code attached to her body. I have my own, and I want yours, or this child dies."

He shook his head. "Is money so important to you that you lose your mind for it?"

"Lose my mind? Of all the people to talk. You...you have people under your toot! People that are literally broke, paying you money they don't even have, making your pockets fat!"

"As you see it, but do you also not see how our land is prosperous? How the people that do work hard never want for anything? Or, do you just see me...what your eyes want you to see, and not your mind? You are a smart man, Tran, but you don't think."

Tran humphed. "Bullshit stop hesitating, give me the codes. You can have the little girl and go back to Laos!"

Vinny Ta turned and started back up the steps.

"Where are you going!"

"Did you not say you wanted the codes?"

"Yeah…but let someone else get them. You stay!" He waved the gun at him.

Vinny Ta glanced up to the entrance of the plane and nodded. "As you wish."

The men that were up there parted and let a woman come through. When Vinny Ta gestured to her, she nodded and disappeared back into the plane.

"Just stay right where you are."

A moment later, right after Ting and his men had made it through into the hanger, Ting yelled out, "Hold it, Tran!"

Tran turned, facing them.

"You double-crossed us!"

"What…what are you talking about? I was going to get the money and share…"

"No, you wanted it for yourself. That's why you tried hiding the money in the first place. Money you were stealing all along!"

"No." He pointed over at Vinny Ta. "He did, he tried to steal your money. Not me! Through the codes…this little girl."

Vinny Ta turned towards Ting and said, "He speaks falsehood, I'm not involved in his corruption."

"No!" He pointed the gun towards them. "He's lying."

Kim and Lui could see that Tran was losing it, and they worried about him hurting Alika. "We need to get Alika out of there."

"Yeah, I see…" Lui pointed toward the back side of the hanger where he'd first seen Tran. He peeked out the door. "There's another door." He turned around, and they backed out the office area and went down aways.

Cold Hard Wind

It was the maintenance workers entrance, and the doorway led to the back end where Tran was right now. Lui opened it slightly, and Kim followed behind. They made it to the next door and ducked down. Lui opened it quietly, and they crept through.

While Lui was still arguing with Ting and Vinny Ta, he came up swiftly behind him and put him in a chokehold. Then batted his hand that held the gun upwards. Kim moved in and grabbed at his arm, twisting with everything she had. The gun dropped, and she picked it up. The grip that Tran had on Alika loosened and Alika rushed to the side out of the way. Kim fell to the side when Tran turned and swung at her. Instead, he caught Lui upside the head, and Lui toppled back some. Tran peeped over on the barrels and spotted a monkey wrench. A huge one, he grabbed it with both hands and swung at Lui, just barely missing him. Lui fell backward in some oil and slid around, he couldn't steady himself. He ended up falling again. Tran was now standing over him and swung. He had a bead directly to his head, but he buckled.

Lui looked over, Ting had shot him. Tran fell to his knees, and Lui rolled over away from him. He tried getting up and when he did, he tried to make a run at Vinny Ta. Vinny Ta didn't move, not an inch. Tran was gunned down before he knew it, not from Vinny Ta's people, but all of Ting's men.

Tran slowly fell forward face down, dead.

Vinny Ta turned toward Ting and asked, "What is your name?"

Ting stepped forward and told him. Vinny Ta looked up at the woman who was up there earlier, and said, "Give her your information."

Ting asked. "No disrespect, but why?"

Vinny Ta patted him on the shoulder and said, "I will need help with the Hip Chong Tong when I get back to Laos. You are the Dai Low…right?"

Ting looked around at his men, and they nodded their heads in approval. Ting then stepped into the plane. Vinny Ta asked his men, "Could you…clean this up for me?"

They moved swiftly, snatching up Tran's body.

Kim had Alika wrapped up in her arms, hugging her. Vinny Ta called Lui over to him, "You know about me, I'm sure."

Lui bowed his head. "About us…me… Alika. Yes, I do! But why did you…"

"I was wrong, forgive me." He pulled him closer. "I will send for your mother and family once I get back."

"But I don't want to go back, I'm okay here." He glanced over at Kim.

"I see, well, I still need you to go with me now. You'll be back soon. There are things you need to know. Things I must show you that only…a Chuk Sut can know."

Lui stared at him. "A Chuk Sut…me?"

"You are my descendant, and I am getting older."

Kim walked over with Alika, and Vinny Ta reached down to hug her. "You will be coming with me, little one." He looked at Kim. "I thank you for all you've done. You shall be greatly rewarded." She beamed and reached out, shaking his hand. Then he glanced over at Lui and winked. "Malana spoke highly of you. You have my blessing and my respect." He turned to him, and Alika walked up the ramp.

Kim turned toward Lui, they embraced and gave each other a long, deep kiss, then Kim said, "Well…this is it, huh?"

"No, I'll be back."

"I'll be here."

Lui kissed her again, and Ting came out of the plane, grinning from ear to ear, carrying a briefcase. He rushed over toward his men, and they all hugged him.

He said, "Now, we have respect." He was now Dai Low or the Hip Chong Tong under blessings from the Chuk Sut.

Afterward, the airport runway crew opened back the hanger and prepared to pull the jet to the runway. But before they did, the plane door stayed open for a while longer. People had to be paid off for the plane's sudden arrival. Kim watched as Alika ran down the ramp stairs toward her.

She jumped in her arms, hugged her and kissed her face. She looked in her eyes and said, "I love you!"

"I love you too, Alika, I always will!" Kim responded.

Lui stuck his head out of the plane and called her, "Alika, let's go! You'll see her again soon, trust me!"

He kissed Kim, and she blew kisses back. The ramp was finally taken away, the plane was shuttled towards the runway and eventually positioned for takeoff. She turned around, realizing she had to make it to the hospital.

Ting asked her, "Do you need a ride?"

Kim smiled at him and said, "Thanks, but no thank you."

"Will you be all right then?"

She looked up at the golden sun going down in the west and walked out toward the runway, looking at the planes taking off. She shivered some from the chill of the Detroit River that bit at her bones and took a deep breath.

"I'll be fine." She turned, looking over toward her old school Wayne State, reminiscing on the times when Malana would invite her up on their dorm roof and watch the sun go down, just the two of them.

Malana would point east and say, *'My people are just getting up now…'* But all she would say back was, *'If that's where you guys come from, you all must have a hell of a cold hard wind.'* Kim laughed, turned and walked off. She didn't understand what she meant then, but she sure as hell did now…It was all about love.

ABOUT THE AUTHOR

I'm Dean Hamid, author with Dean Hamid Presents. I'm somewhat of an old-school type of guy. Been around for a while, I mean, not in regards to eBooks, etc., but writing. Different schools of thought in regards to the craft and all. I'm born and raised in Brooklyn, Williamsburg, Bushwick, and Bed-Stuy. I went to an Art and Design high school in NYC. I studied broadcasting, I'm also a military vet. I've been a husband, and I'm a father. All these things have shaped me into the man I am, and in all actual the books I write.

I made the decision to become a published author because I believed then as I do now, that I can do what a guy like Stephen Spielberg, David Baldacci does, or even Dean Koontz, and write good stories like them. I corresponded with many authors back in the day, before the eBook phase, and I believed I could be just as successful as they are.

I would like to do more mysteries, suspense, and keep writing action-thriller dramas. However, I would definitely want to stay with urban but not necessarily African-American.

I have no desire to tell of the initial hand to mouth of the street hustlers and gangsters. I'd like to delve more into what made it come about, and the whole thought and drive that pushes criminal behavior and criminal hustling. The inward thoughts and mindset.

That's the realities of what I saw growing up. That's the story I want to tell.